FUNNY STORIES FOR
SEVEN YEAR OLDS

Helen Paiba is known as one of the most committed, knowledgeable and acclaimed children's booksellers in Britain. For more than twenty years she owned and ran the Children's Bookshop in Muswell Hill, London, which under her guidance gained a superb reputation for its range of children's books and for the advice available to its customers.

Helen was involved with the Booksellers Association for many years and served on both its Children's Bookselling Group and the Trade Practices Committee. In 1995 she was given honorary life membership of the Booksellers Association of Great Britain and Ireland in recognition of her outstanding services to the association and to the book trade. In the same year the Children's Book Circle (sponsored by Books for Children) honoured her with the Eleanor Farjeon Award, given for distinguished service to the world of children's books.

She retired and now lives in London.

Funny
STORIES

FOR SEVEN YEAR OLDS

COMPILED BY HELEN PAIBA

ILLUSTRATED BY ALAN SNOW

MACMILLAN CHILDREN'S BOOKS

For the children of
Muswell Hill past and present
who helped to inspire me. H.P.

First published 1998 by Macmillan Children's Books
a division of Macmillan Publishers Limited
25 Eccleston Place, London SW1W 9NF
Basingstoke and Oxford
www.macmillan.com

Associated companies throughout the world

ISBN 0 330 349457

13 15 17 19 18 16 14

A CIP catalogue record for this book is available
from the British Library.

Typeset by SX Composing DTP, Rayleigh, Essex
Printed and bound in Great Britain by
Mackays of Chatham plc, Kent

Contents

The Downhill Crocodile Whizz

Margaret Mahy

One day a small crocodile received an unexpected present for his last birthday but one. It was from his grandmother who was away somewhere leading a very sprightly life of her own. The crocodile felt the parcel all over, trying to guess what might be inside it.

"She's sent me shoes," said the crocodile in a slightly disappointed voice. But it was not shoes. It was a pair of roller skates and a letter.

"Dear Grandson," said the letter, "I am sending you my old roller skates because I am giving up skating and taking up

1

hang-gliding instead. Look after these skates very well, won't you, because they are good ones. On these very skates I won the Ladies All-in Skating Championship of Orinocco. I am afraid you will never be the skater that I am, but you might as well have a go. Happy birthday for your last birthday but one. Your devoted Grandmother." Then at the very end of the letter it said, "PTO" which stands for *Please Turn Over*, but the crocodile did not notice this.

"What does she mean, I'll never be the skater that she is?" he cried. "Great Granglenuckers! As if I couldn't skate better that an old woman crocodile of ninety-two." He dropped the letter and began studying the skates. "I see. You strap them on to your paws. Simple!"

He put the skates on straight away and stood up very confidently. Then he had to stand up all over again. Next he shot across the room and found he was lying on his back with the skates in the air.

"Funny!" mused the crocodile. "I wonder how that happened?"

At last he managed to stand up and stay standing up, balancing cleverly with his tail.

"There you are . . . Easy!" said the crocodile in rather a bruised voice. "Now I'm going to have a go outside. Somehow I have the feeling I'm going to be a singularly splendid skater."

As it happened, the crocodile lived at the very top of a very steep hill. There was absolutely nowhere to go in any direction but DOWN. So the crocodile pointed his feet, in his grandmother's skates, in the direction of

down . . . simply to have a go. WHIZZZZ! Off he went, balancing majestically with his fine tail.

It's easy! thought the crocodile. I don't see what all the fuss is about. The skates do it all for you. He went faster and faster. WHIZZZ!

A little girl called Katy was sitting in front of her gate on a tricycle. Her mother had told her never to go out of the gate because of the steepness of the hill outside, but when she saw the crocodile going past, she couldn't resist joining in too.

WHIZZZ! went the crocodile. WHIZZZZZ! went Katy.

"Isn't this fun?" yelled Katy. "I'll stop when you do."

"I don't think I'll be stopping for a while," the crocodile cried in an anxious voice. "I've just found out that these skates aren't the sort of skates that have brakes." They went faster and faster. Two dogs were pulling a rubbish bag to pieces, but they stopped to watch Katy and the crocodile go by.

"*They're* having fun," barked Black Dog.

"Let's go along too, shall we?" said Spotted Dog. "This rubbish bag is a very disappointing one." So the two dogs joined in too, wagging their tails and waving their tongues as they ran. WHIZZZZ! WHIZZZZZ! WAG! WAG!

When they were further down the hill they came across rich old Mr Whisker tucked into his wheelchair, being wheeled across the footpath to his car by his dashing nurse who was called Nurse Frolic. A chauffeur was holding the car door open and bowing, but unfortunately as Katy and the crocodile whizzed by they brushed against the wheelchair which spun round three times and then joined them in the downhill whizz-and-wag procession.

"Isn't this fun?" Katy called to Mr Whisker.

"Hooray! Here we go!" he shouted most enthusiastically, glad to get away from Nurse Frolic and the chauffeur who were both very bossy and always said they were only bossy for his own good.

"I'm going to stop when the crocodile stops," shouted Katy.

"So am I!" agreed Mr Whisker. "These crocodiles know a thing or two."

"I won't be stopping immediately," mumbled the crocodile desperately, balancing with his tail for all he was worth and making circles in the air with his short front legs.

"Isn't he clever?" yapped Black Dog.

"Yes," panted Spotted Dog. "He keeps pretending he's going to fall over and then he never quite does."

They went faster and faster, while behind them, shouting and yelling, ran Katy's mother, Nurse Frolic and the chauffeur.

About halfway down the hill they came upon Mrs Harris leaning out of the window and telling her husband which apples to buy at the greengrocer's.

She was holding their baby – a fine boy named Sampson.

"Not those green ones," she was saying, "and not the very red ones . . ."

But just then she heard a whizzing sound and saw the crocodile, Katy, Mr Whisker, Black Dog, Spotted Dog – thirteen wheels and eight paws – all speeding towards her.

She got a terrible fright.

"Awwwk!' she screamed and – dropped the baby.

Luckily, as the crocodile shot under her window, waving his short little arms, he just happened to catch little Sampson and carried him off at great speed.

WHIZZZ! went the crocodile and Sampson. WHIZZZ! went Katy. WHIZZZZ! went Mr Whisker. WAG-WAG went Black Dog. WAG-WAG went Spotted Dog. "Stop! Stop! STOP! STOP!" shouted Katy's mother, Nurse Frolic, the chauffeur and the Harrises who joined in, running faster than the others because they were so upset to see their baby carried off by a crocodile.

A brass band in a bus turned into the road on its way down to the park at the bottom of the hill where it was going to play that very afternoon.

"Look! A downhill crocodile whizz!" exclaimed the bandmaster, leaping from his seat and reaching for his baton. "Let's give them a bit of an oom pah pah! Ready, boys? *Prestissimo accelerando!*"

The band began to play *Land of Hope and Glory* with all the *prestissimo* and *accelerando* that a heart could desire. They opened the windows for the trombones and the driver speeded up a little bit so that they could keep up with the crocodile who, by now, was going downhill very fast indeed.

Up in a tall building in the heart of the city, a military man called General Confusion was pacing up and down impatiently. Every now and then he looked out of the window, swore, and went back to his impatience and his pacing. It was years and years and years since there had been a war and he was very cross about it. He had had a grand uniform and a whole army for years and years, and absolutely nothing had happened. Then, as he looked out of the window he thought he saw something ominous whizzing down the hill as if it were about to launch an attack on the park gates.

"Enemies! At last!" shouted General Confusion. "We are being invaded." Then he took his brass bugle, leaned out of the window, and blew a gallant blast on it.

Taranta ra! Taranta ra! Out rushed the majors and the captains, and the sergeant majors, and the ordinary soldiers – all armed with bazookas and blunderbusses and ready for battle and bloodshed.

"FORWARD!" shouted the General. "Defend the bottom of the hill! Protect the gates of our lovely civic park!" As one soldier the army charged towards the bottom of the hill.

"There goes the army!" everyone said. "There's going to be a battle." There was great excitement, and everyone held up their babies and aged parents so that they could get a good view too. WHIZZZZ! went the crocodile. He was going so fast that he was absolutely numb with terror. Katy followed behind him, and everyone else just after her.

"Aren't you ever going to stop?" Katy shouted to the crocodile.

"Er . . ." said the crocodile.

"Look at him!" yelled Mr Whisker, waving his hearing aid with admiration. "He's skating on one foot . . . now he's skating on the other. What a croc, what a croc, what a crackerjack croc!"

"They're waiting for us," cried Katy. "We've become famous since we started off at the top of the hill."

"Do you think we'd better stop?" asked Mr Whisker. "We're going very fast. We don't want to run into anyone, and cause an accident."

But the crocodile couldn't stop. WHIZZZZ! went his grandmother's All-in-Champion-of-Orinocco skates. He swayed this way. He swayed that way. He balanced with his tail, and he tried to think what to do next. But there was only one thing he *could* do! Holding little Sampson high in the air to save him from any bumps and bruises, he shouted, "Follow me!" and they did follow him, all of them.

WHIZZZZ! He whizzed right through the ranks of soldiers. The bazookas went one way and the blunderbusses went another. Luckily the park gates were open and the crocodile went right through the gates at about a hundred kilometres an hour, and then three times around the park, holding little Sampson Harris, who gurgled with delight and patted the crocodile's long, leathery snout. They were followed by Katy, Mr Whisker, Black Dog, Spotted Dog, Mr and Mrs Harris, Nurse Frolic, the chauffeur, Katy's mother, and a brass band in a bus playing like men inspired. People cheered, and so did their babies and their aged parents. It was the most interesting and inspiring incident to have taken place in that town for some time.

At last the crocodile was able to stop. He was quite out of breath what with trying to balance and looking after little Sampson Harris as well. But before he had time to settle down a bit, General Confusion was surrounding him with bruised soldiers and dented bazookas.

"Arrest that wicked crocodile!" he roared, pointing at the crocodile with his sword.

"No, don't!" cried another voice. "Don't you dare lay a finger on that noble creature. That dear reptile has saved the life of our little Sampson."

"What?" cried General Confusion, suddenly noticing the baby. "He's saved the life of our little Sampson? What a spirited saurian! What a croc, what a croc, what crackerjack croc!"

For Mrs Harris, before she had married Mr Harris, had been the beautiful Miss Confusion, the General's own daughter, and so Sampson was the General's own grandson.

So the unexpected downhill crocodile whizz became an unexpected park party. Everyone had a lovely time, including the babies and the aged parents. The band played fit to bust, and the General pinned one of his medals on to the crocodile's waistcoat. Mr Whisker (who was *very* rich) said he would pay to have a bronze statue put up in the park, showing the crocodile balancing on one skate and catching baby Sampson in his short little arms.

Then Mr and Mrs Harris took Sampson home and General Confusion took the army home, Katy's mother took Katy home, Nurse Frolic and the chauffeur took Mr Whisker home, and the band took their bassoons and trombones home. And everyone else took their babies and aged parents and went home too.

But there was nobody to take the crocodile home. After slapping him on the back and waving goodbye, everybody left the crocodile standing in his grandmother's skates in the golden evening light.

That's all right! he thought. I'll skate home. It won't take long.

But he *couldn't* skate home. It was uphill all the way.

He had to walk uphill on his short little legs. Black Dog and Spotted Dog went with him most of the way, but then they saw a very promising rubbish bag and forgot about the crocodile who was all plodding and slow now. He wasn't nearly as much fun going uphill as he had been coming down.

At last the crocodile staggered in through his own front door at the very top of the hill, dead beat, dog tired and done for. He collapsed into a chair and sat still for a long time, just breathing and blinking, breathing and blinking. Then he noticed his grandmother's birthday letter still on the table, and he saw that at the very end of the birthday letter she had written PTO which (as you know) means *Please Turn Over*. So the crocodile picked it up and PTO-ed.

"Dear Grandson," his grandmother had written on the other side of the page. "Whatever you do, WATCH OUT FOR HILLS! Your loving Grandmother."

Clever Stan and the Stupid Dragon

Retold by Stephen Corrin

Why was Stan Bolovan an unhappy man? He had a comfortable house, two healthy cows and a garden with lots of fruit trees. Well, it was his wife. She was *always* crying. And I mean always. In the morning, after dinner, after supper and even when it was time to go to bed. In other respects she was quite a good sort, really.

You might have thought that she would have told Stan (who was a good husband) *why* she was always crying. But no. She would not tell him. "Leave me alone," she would say. "You wouldn't understand, even if I did tell you." But he kept on pestering her day after day, week after week, month after month, until at last, one fine day, she *did* tell him. "I keep crying," she said tearfully, "because we haven't got any children." When Stan heard this, he too became all sad and miserable, and so the Bolovan household wasn't a very cheerful place, I can tell you.

Stan decided to consult a magician. The magician gazed long into the crystal globe and said not a word. Stan waited and waited until at last he became impatient.

"Come on," he said, "I want your help. Say something."

The magician looked up at him. "Are you quite certain you want children?" he asked. "They can be a great burden, you know."

"Yes, I know," said Stan, "but what a happy burden; it's the kind of burden my wife and I are dying to have."

"Very well then," said the magician, "you shall have your wish."

Stan left with a light heart and started back on his journey home (for he had come a long way to see the magician). He was longing to tell his wife the good news. "How marvellous!" he thought. "There'll be no more crying from now on, not from my wife at any rate."

Imagine his surprise, when he reached the door of his house, at hearing the sound of children's voices laughing and chattering, and little feet pattering all over the place. He went round into the garden and a wonderful sight met his eyes. There were dozens and dozens of children of all shapes and sizes, fat ones and thin ones, tall ones and short ones, children with fair hair and blue eyes and children with dark hair and brown eyes, children with curls and children with straight hair, quiet children and noisy children, cheeky children and shy children – in fact every imaginable variety.

"Good heavens," said Stan Bolovan to his wife, "there must be at least a hundred children here!"

"And every one of them welcome," smiled his wife.

"But how on earth are we going to clothe and feed them all?" asked Stan, perplexed. But his wife only went on smiling. He soon found that she had given all the milk and all the fruit to the children and there wasn't a morsel of food left in the house.

So Stan Bolovan set out to find food and clothing for his children.

After walking for nearly a whole day, he espied a shepherd who was herding his many sheep and lambs in a field.

"I know it's the wrong thing to do," thought poor Stan Bolovan, "but if I wait till it's dark I might be able to get a lamb or two and feed my hungry children with some juicy meat." He hid behind a stout oak tree and waited for night to fall. Suddenly, round about midnight, he heard a great whirring, rushing sound in the skies and lo and behold! he looked up and saw a dragon swooping from a great height straight down among the sheep. It picked up a lamb in each of its four paws and flew up again.

The poor old shepherd was running all over the place, trying to keep his fear-crazed flock together and Stan Bolovan decided to help him. At last, when they had restored some sort of order, they sat down against a tree to rest.

"You know," sighed the shepherd, "this happens every single night. If things go on like this I soon won't have a sheep to my name." He thanked Stan for his help and offered him some bread and cheese. This made Stan feel very much better.

"What will you give me," he asked, "if I rid you of that dragon?"

"I'll give you as much food and drink as you like, as well as three rams, three sheep and three lambs."

"That's a bargain," said Stan, not having the slightest idea how he was going to conquer the dragon.

He spent the next day helping the shepherd and thinking about his hungry brood of children. As night drew on, a great dread seized him and it was all he could do to stop himself shaking and shivering with fear.

At midnight the air was suddenly filled with the fierce whirring and rushing sound and the fearsome dragon, his scales gleaming in the moonlight, came swooping down amid the sheep.

Stan Bolovan, feeling quite crazily bold, stood up and bawled, "Stop! Stop at once!"

The beast, quite taken aback, sank slowly to the ground.

"And may I enquire to whom I 'ave the *h*onour of speakin'?" he said somewhat breathlessly.

"I am Stan Bolovan. Stan Bolovan the Mighty, eater-up of rocks and gobbler of mountains. One move from you towards those sheep and I'll gobble *you* up."

The dragon, for want of anything better to say, muttered grimly: "You'll have to fight me first."

"Please don't invite me to fight you," said Stan Bolovan. "I'd kill you with one breath and your corpse would be a nice filling for my sandwiches."

The dragon was a terrible coward at heart.

"Well, I've got to be goin' now," he said. "I'll bid ye goodnight."

"Steady on," said Stan, "we've got an account to settle first, haven't we now?"

"What? What? What account?" asked the dragon nervously.

"Those sheep you've been stealing every night," said Stan Bolovan. "They are my sheep, you know. That man over there is a shepherd who works for me. You'd better settle up here and now, or there'll be trouble."

The dragon, of course, had no money on him and he had no wish to be made into filling for Stan's sandwiches, so he said: "My old mother has stacks and stacks of money. Come and stay with us for three or four days and help her about the house. If she likes you, she'll give you ten sacks of gold every day."

"Very well," said Stan Bolovan, getting bolder and bolder every minute. "Lead me to her." He thought what a lot of food and clothing ten sacks of gold would buy for his hundred children. "I'll face the old dragoness even if it kills me."

So off they went to the dragon's residence and found the dragon's mother waiting outside the door. Her first words were not terribly encouraging. "What!" she shrieked, her scales standing up in fury. "No sheep!"

"Sh!" said the dragon soothingly. "I've brought you a visitor." And to Stan he whispered: "Don't worry, I'll go and explain."

Stan waited outside. He could hear the dragon's quite audible whispers: "This chap's a terror; he devours rocks and mountains and uses dead dragons as filling for his sandwiches."

"Leave him to me," said the mother dragon, not even bothering to lower her voice. "*I'll* see to him."

They called Stan in and showed him to a great bed where he was to sleep for the night. But he hardly had a wink of sleep. He kept having nightmares about the mother dragon with her bulging green eyes and ugly back scales.

Next morning she said to Stan: "Let me see whether you really are stronger than my son." And she picked up an enormous metal barrel bound round with iron hoops. The dragon took hold of it and hurled it with all his might and Stan heard it crash into the ground at what seemed like miles and miles away. He and the dragon walked after it and found it buried in the earth of a mountain-side about three miles off.

"Your turn," said the dragon. Stan Bolovan, playing for time, looked down at it and sighed.

"Well, what are ye waitin' for?" asked the dragon.

"I'm just thinking," began Stan slowly. "What a pity it would be if I had to kill you with this beautiful barrel."

"What d'ye mean?" asked the dragon.

"Well, just take a look at my hands," answered Stan, holding out his hands with fingers outspread, as though there was something special about them. "D'you see those magnetic veins? Anything I throw *always comes back*, and if this barrel should collide with your head in passing, there'd be one nice cracked dragon's skull lying around."

"Oh," said the dragon nervously. "There's no great hurry for you to have your turn just yet. Let's have something to eat first. I'm feeling hungry." And he went back to his house and brought back great stacks of food and they both sat down and ate their fill, right up till evening when the moon came up.

"Well," said Stan Bolovan, standing up and stretching himself. "I suppose I ought to have my throw now, but I'd better wait till the moon goes down in the sky, because if the barrel happens to land on the moon, it's liable to get stuck there for ever. You wouldn't want to lose it, would you?"

"Oh no," said the dragon hastily. "It's me mother's favourite barrel. Better not risk throwing it yet. In fact, better not throw it at all, in case it gets stuck on some planet or other."

"But I must," protested Stan Bolovan. "Your mother distinctly said I must. It's a test of strength, remember?"

"I'll tell ye what," proposed the dragon. "Let *me* throw it back towards the house. I'll make it go farther this time and I'll tell her that you did it. Then you'll have beaten me, and Mother will never know a thing."

"No!" replied Stan Bolovan. "No! No! No!"

But when the dragon offered him twenty sacks of gold not to throw the barrel, he said:

"Oh, very well, if you feel so strongly about it . . ."

Then the dragon returned to the house and told his mother that Stan had beaten him once again and had thrown the barrel a good mile further than he had. "Oh dearie me," said the mother and she began to feel rather scared.

But by next morning she had another plan to get rid of Stan Bolovan.

"Go and fetch me water from the spring," she said giving them twenty big buffalo skins. "Let's see which of you can carry most in one day."

The dragon started first and went backwards and forwards from his house to the spring and from the spring to the house till he had filled and emptied all twenty skins. He then handed them to Stan.

"Your turn," he said.

Instead of taking them Stan took a knife out of his pocket, bent down and began scratching the earth near the spring.

"What on earth are ye up to now?" asked the dragon suspiciously.

"I want to get at this spring," replied Stan. "Then I'll carry the whole lot of water in one go. Seems a terrible waste of time going to and fro with those tiny buffalo skins."

"N-n-no," said the dragon nervously. "You mustn't do that. That spring belongs to the local dragon family. It was originally made by my great-great-great-grandfather. Keep your hands off it, please. I'll carry the skins for you in half the time I did it. Mother will be none the wiser."

"No," said Stan firmly, and went on digging.

Finally the dragon had to promise him yet another twenty sacks of gold before he could get him to stop. And so the dragon did all the to-ing and fro-ing with the skins, rushing like mad to get it finished before the day was over, while Stan lay resting on his great bed.

The mother dragon got more and more scared on learning that her son had been beaten yet again, but by the next morning she had thought of another plan.

They were told to go to collect wood in the forest, to see which of them would get more.

The dragon immediately began wrenching out great oaks as if they were no bigger than matchsticks and arranged them neatly in rows. But Stan climbed to the top of a tree that had a long creeper trailing round it. With this creeper he tied the top of the tree he was sitting on to the top of the next tree.

"I'm tying all these trees together," he explained to the dragon. "Then I'll be able to clear the whole forest at one go."

"No! Please no!" wailed the dragon, his scales visibly shrinking with fear. "My great-great-great-great-grandfather planted this forest. Please, please don't."

"Sorry about that," said Stan Bolovan, "but I'm not going to trudge to and fro with a mere half dozen trees at a time."

So the dragon had to promise yet another twenty sacks of gold before Stan finally said, "Oh very well, if you insist . . ."

The dragons, mother and son, now decided they had had enough and told Stan they would give him another hundred sacks of gold if he would go away and leave them in peace.

Stan, of course, was only too delighted. But how was he going to carry all those heavy sacks of gold back to his house? That night, as he lay awake in his giant bed thinking how to solve this problem, he heard the voices of the mother dragon and her son.

"We shall be ruined," the mother was saying, "we'll have nothing left."

"Well, what is there we can do about it?" the son asked in a rather weak and helpless tone of voice.

"There's only one thing we can do," replied the mother. "You must *kill* him this very night."

"*Me* kill 'im?" exclaimed the son. "It's 'im who'll kill me, more likely."

"Not if you listen to your mother he won't," said she. "Now just wait till he's fast asleep, then go in and bash his head with great-grandfather's club."

"Aha!" thought Stan Bolovan. "So that's what they're up to!"

He crept quietly out of bed and went outside to the yard where the pigs' trough was. He filled it with earth and dragged it in on to his bed and covered it with blankets. He himself got under the bed and snored as noisily as he could.

Soon he heard the dragon tiptoe into the room, stop by the bedside and bring down the club with a deafening thwack on to the trough. Stan stopped snoring and let out a long-drawn-out groan, as though he were dying. Shortly afterwards he crept out from under the bed and dragged the trough back to its place in the yard, leaving his bed nice and tidy.

When the dragon and his mother beheld Stan next morning, they could hardly believe their eyes.

"G-g-g-good mornin'," said the dragon. "'Ope you slept well on your last night here."

"I slept fine," replied Stan, "just fine. There was a fly or something that crawled over my nose and tickled me rather, but otherwise I slept just fine. So fine, in fact, that I think I'll stay here another night, if you don't mind. It's not all that often I get the chance to sleep in such a comfy bed."

Both mother and son looked so distinctly

uncomfortable when they heard this that Stan continued: "Well, if I'm really all that unwelcome, I'll leave today. I don't wish to be a burden . . . but on one condition."

"Any condition, any condition," said both dragons hastily in unison. "You name it."

"You must carry all the sacks of gold back to my house for me. It'd look a bit undignified for the mighty Stan Bolovan to be seen lugging sacks around."

The dragon was only too eager to comply. He picked up the sacks in his great claws and flung them on to his enormous back.

"Well, I'll say cheeri-ho," said Stan to the mother dragon, "and thanks for everything."

"Not at all, not at all," she replied and hurriedly locked the door behind him.

Stan and the dragon began their long journey back home. After a trek lasting many hours, Stan could hear the sound of his children's voices in the distance.

He stopped and turned to the dragon.

"Those are my children playing and shouting. I shouldn't think you'd care to meet them. There's about a hundred of them

– all just about as strong as I am, and they can be very rough sometimes. Perhaps you'd . . ." But before he could finish his sentence, the dragon had dropped the sacks and fled in terror. He didn't fancy the thought of meeting a hundred young Stan Bolovans!

Just at that moment Stan's wife came out to greet him, following by the enormous brood of laughing, jolly children.

There was enough gold in the sacks to feed and clothe them for the rest of their lives.

Cup Final

Margaret Joy

"**G**uess what – it's the first Saturday in May next week," said Dad.

"Oh yes?" said Mum.

"Cup Final Day," said Dad.

"Oh," said Mum. "So I suppose you'll be sitting in a darkened room all day with beer and crisps and the television?"

"Only from eleven onwards," said Dad. "That's when they start reporting from Wembley: the weather, the state of the turf, the team members, the ref—"

"All right, all right," cried Mum. "The same as last year and the year before that and the year before that – though how you can bear to sit watching from eleven in the morning, when the game itself doesn't start until three, I just don't understand."

She turned to Foxy.

"And I suppose you'll be glued to the box as well?"

Foxy just grinned at her.

That Saturday Dad was up early. There was a feeling of excitement and expectancy in the air. Gran and Mum were going to town for the day, taking Betsy with them.

"When will you be back?" asked Dad.

"Oh, about six, I expect," said Mum.

"But you'll miss the whole thing," he said. "And the presentation of the Cup and medals and everything."

"That's the idea," said Mum and Gran together.

Before they set off on the bus, Mum said: "Now you don't really mind being left alone all day, do you? You know we're not a scrap interested in football."

Dad assured them that he didn't mind in the least – in fact, he preferred to be left to enjoy the occasion in peace. He waved them off absent-mindedly, then settled down to arrange everything just as he wanted it. The television set was to face his armchair, with a table at his right hand for refreshments; he also had the double-page sports spread from the paper for handy reference. By ten to eleven he was sitting ready, with his United rosette pinned to his pullover. The curtains were closed and the room was dim except for the television screen. In his imagination he was already standing on the terraces at Wembley.

Foxy wasn't really interested in the build-up to the Final; he only wanted to watch the game itself. He put his head round the door and hissed: "I'm just going round to Imran's. I'll be back in time for the kick-off."

"Right – ssshhh," nodded his dad. "See you later."

The two boys had a good morning together until Imran's mum called him in for a meal. She said to Foxy: "Shouldn't you be going for yours now?"

Foxy explained about its being Cup Final day. She tutted sympathetically.

"So you're a football orphan, are you? Poor Foxy. Then you'd better stay and have something with us. It's lucky we're having elastic curry today."

"Elastic curry?" said Foxy.

"Yes," she smiled. "It can always stretch for one more."

Foxy really enjoyed it; he had been expecting to share a snack with his dad. But he was still keeping his eye on the time.

"That was great," he said at half past two. "But I think I'd better be getting back now."

"Won't you have another helping of ice cream?" asked Imran's mum.

"No, thanks," said Foxy. "I must go. Dad's expecting me."

"Off you go then," she said. "I know the kick-off is at three – you'd better not miss that."

Foxy ran all the way home. He dashed into the house and sat down, panting, his eyes already fixed on the television. The players were lined up in the middle of the Wembley pitch.

"You're just in time," said Dad. "The Duke's just going to shake hands with them."

"Look, he's going to the Rovers first," said Foxy.

"Don't they look a load of thugs and ruffians?" cried Dad in disgust.

"Now he's going to United."

"Great lads!" exclaimed Dad. "Don't they look fighting fit? What a team!"

The ref blew his whistle.

"United have the ball," cried Foxy.

"Come on now, boys," said Dad. "Get stuck in there!"

Both teams went into the attack. The ball thudded this way and that, there were fast passes across the field, and some clever footwork and tackling, as well as some skilful dribbling up the sidelines – but all attempts at goal shots were headed off by the defenders of both teams. To and fro, to and fro, minute after minute. It was very frustrating for everyone, but the teams were evenly matched. When the half-time whistle blew, there was still no score. Dad groaned in despair.

"I don't know if I can stand any more of this," he said – but he didn't mean it. "I tell you what, Foxy, just so I don't miss anything, will you do me a favour?"

He dug his hand into his pocket for change.

"Run to the shop and get four more packets of crisps and half a dozen sausage rolls."

Foxy raced down the road to the shop on the corner. Two other customers were already there. He jigged impatiently from foot to foot while they chatted to the shopkeeper. At last one of the women saw Foxy's face.

"You'd better serve this little 'un first," she said. "He looks as though he's on pins to get back to the football – am I right?"

Foxy nodded and stammered out: "F-four packets of c-crisps and six s-sausage rolls, please."

As the shopkeeper counted out the sausage rolls, he called back over his shoulder to Foxy: "Salt and vinegar, ready salted, cheese and onion or barbecue beef?"

"Oh, er, the first four you come to," said Foxy.

The minutes of half-time were ticking away. He bit his lip anxiously.

"Come on, come *on*," he thought.

The shopkeeper seemed to be working in slow motion. At last, Foxy had the change in his pocket and was cradling the bag of sausage rolls and the packets of crisps in his arms. He made for the shop door. The woman opened it for him with a smile.

"Hope your team wins," she said.

But Foxy didn't hear. He was thundering down the street and skidding in at the gate. His dad had left the front door open for him.

"Come on, quick," called Dad. "They're just starting again."

Foxy slumped on to the settee. His heart was pumping wildly and he was prickly with sweat. He tore off his pullover.

"Here," said Dad, and handed him a glass of lemonade.

"Great," said Foxy, and drank it straight off.

His dad refilled the glass and Foxy gulped half of that down too.

"Can you turn the sound up a bit?" said his dad.

Foxy put his glass on top of the set while he adjusted the volume.

39

"Better?" he asked.

"Mmm," nodded his dad, his eyes fixed on the screen. "Here they go again, they've got the ball – come on now, United."

He leant forward, urging them on.

"Look, Smithy's got the ball now."

Smithy was United's amazing goal scorer – if anyone could get a goal, it was Smithy.

"Phew, I'm still boiling," said Foxy, bending down to unlace his trainers.

"Out to the wing – to Jackson!" yelled Dad. "Now back to Smithy!"

Foxy put one foot behind the other and eased off one of his trainers. His foot was so sweaty that the trainer wouldn't come off. He gave it a sharp jerk to loosen it.

"Run, Smithy! – the man's got two false legs – get a move on, RUN!"

At that moment Foxy's trainer, loosened at last, hurtled through the air and hit the glass of lemonade on top of the television. Smithy was racing towards an opening in Rovers' defence and pulled back his foot to shoot –

But the screen went blank as lemonade poured down inside the set. There was a sudden hissing noise and a cloud of steam rose in the air. There was a burning smell – and the screen stayed blank. Foxy couldn't move a muscle for sheer horror at what he had done.

"FOXY!" yelled his father.

He leapt forward and twiddled all the knobs, but there was no sound and no picture. He unplugged the set at the mains and raced into the kitchen to find the tranny.

"I don't believe this is happening, this can't be true," he cried. "Was it a goal or not? I've got to find out, are they a goal ahead or not?"

The tranny was tuned into Mum's favourite station, not the sports commentary. He twiddled the tuning knob this way and that, but there seemed to be nothing but music.

"I can't find the blessed thing," he groaned. "Surely *someone* at the BBC knows the Cup Final's on."

The tranny needed new batteries, and soon what sound there was, had faded away. Dad looked desperately at his watch.

"It must be nearly over," he said wildly.

"I've got to find out what's happening. I know – old Porrett'll be watching – he'll let me see the last few minutes."

He raced out into the street, shot across the road to Mr Porrett's and banged on the door. Poor Foxy hadn't moved. He was still looking helplessly at the steam fizzing gently from the television. He glanced at his feet – one trainer was still on, the other was lying behind the set next to pieces of broken glass in a pool of lemonade . . .

Soon afterwards, the others returned from town, loaded down with carrier bags, noisy and cheerful. They found the house strangely silent. Foxy and his dad were both kneeling behind the television set. Foxy was carefully picking up pieces of glass; Dad was trying to dry the carpet and the back of the set with Mum's hairdryer.

"What on earth are you doing back there?" asked Gran. "There's no picture at *that* side of the set, you know."

Dad snarled something that Gran couldn't hear. He was still angry with Mr Porrett for not being in.

"Guess what happened to us," said Mum brightly. "We were just walking through the shopping precinct, and there was this crowd of people looking in a shop window. They were looking into a showroom, watching television. Well, you know we're not normally a bit interested in the Cup Final, but anyway, we stopped and watched for a bit, didn't we, Gran? – and we saw the last few minutes of the match."

"Yes," said Gran. "It was really exciting, wasn't it?"

Dad gritted his teeth; Foxy wished he was ten miles away.

"Wasn't that goal of Smithy's fantastic?" said Mum. "That man really is magic, isn't he? Still, I don't need to tell you two that: I expect you've been glued to the set ever since we left, haven't you? Did you ever see a goal like it?"

"No," said Dad and Foxy together. "No, never."

Paddington Goes Underground

Michael Bond

Paddington was very surprised when he woke up and found himself in bed. He decided it was a nice feeling as he stretched himself and pulled the sheets up round his head with a paw. He reached out with his feet and found a cool spot for his toes. One advantage of being a very small bear in a large bed was that there was so much room.

After a few minutes he poked his head out cautiously. and sniffed. There was a lovely smell of something coming under the door. It seemed to be getting nearer and nearer. There were footsteps too, coming up the stairs. As they stopped by his door there was a knock and Mrs Bird's voice called out, "Are you awake, young Paddington?"

"Only just," called out Paddington, rubbing his eyes.

The door opened. "You've had a good sleep," said Mrs Bird as she placed a tray on the bed and drew the curtains. "And you're a very privileged person to have breakfast in bed on a *weekday*!"

Paddington eyed the tray hungrily. There was half a grapefruit in a bowl, a plate of bacon and eggs, some toast, and a whole pot of marmalade, not to mention a large cup of tea. "Is that all for me?" he exclaimed.

"If you don't want it I can soon take it away again," said Mrs Bird.

"Oh, I do," said Paddington, hurriedly. "It's just that I've never seen so much breakfast before."

"Well, you'd better hurry up with it." Mrs Bird turned in the doorway and looked back. "Because you're going on a shopping expedition this morning with Mrs Brown and Judy. And all I can say is, thank goodness I'm not going too!" She closed the door.

"Now I wonder what she meant by that?" said Paddington. But he didn't worry about it for very long. There was far too much to do. It was the first time he had ever had breakfast in bed and he soon found it wasn't quite so easy as it looked. First of all he had trouble with the grapefruit. Every time he pressed it with his spoon a long stream of juice shot up and hit him in the eye, which was very painful. And all the time he was worried because the bacon and eggs were getting cold. Then there was the question of the marmalade. He wanted to leave room for the marmalade.

In the end he decided it would be easier if he mixed everything up on one plate and sat on the tray to eat it.

"Oh, Paddington," said Judy when she entered the room a few minutes later and found him perched on the tray, "whatever are you doing now? Do hurry up. We're waiting for you downstairs."

Paddington looked up, an expression of bliss on his face; that part of his face which could be seen behind eggy whiskers and toast crumbs. He tried to say something but all he could manage was a muffled grunting noise which sounded like IMJUSTCOMING all rolled into one.

"Really!" Judy took out her handkerchief and wiped his face. "You're the stickiest bear imaginable. And if you don't hurry up all the nice things will be gone. Mummy's going to buy you a complete new outfit at Barkridges – I heard her say so. Now, comb your fur quickly and come on down."

As she closed the door Paddington looked at the remains of his breakfast. Most of it was gone but there was a large piece of bacon left which it seemed a pity to waste. He decided to put it in his suitcase in case he got hungry later on.

He hurried into the bathroom and rubbed his face over with some warm water. Then he combed his whiskers carefully and a few moments later, not looking perhaps as clean as he had done the evening before, but quite smart, he arrived downstairs.

"I hope you're not wearing that hat," said Mrs Brown, as she looked down at him.

"Oh, do let him, Mummy," cried Judy. "It's so . . . unusual."

"It's unusual all right," said Mrs Brown. "I don't know that I've ever seen anything quite like it before. It's such a funny shape. I don't know what you'd call it."

"It's a bush hat," said Paddington, proudly. "And it saved my life."

"Saved your life?" repeated Mrs Brown. "Don't be silly. How could a hat save your life?"

Paddington was about to tell her of his adventure in the bath the evening before when he received a nudge from Judy. "Er . . . it's a long story," he said, lamely.

"Then you'd better save it for another time," said Mrs Brown. "Now, come along, both of you."

Paddington picked up his suitcase and followed Mrs Brown and Judy to the front door. By the door Mrs Brown paused and sniffed.

"That's very strange," she said. "There seems to be a smell of bacon everywhere this morning. Can *you* smell it, Paddington?"

Paddington started. He put the suitcase guiltily behind himself and sniffed. He had several expressions which he kept for emergencies. There was his thoughtful expression, when he stared into space and rested his chin on a paw. Then there was his innocent one which wasn't really an expression at all. He decided to use this one.

"It's very strong," he said truthfully, for he was a truthful bear. And then he added, perhaps not quite so truthfully, "I wonder where it's coming from?"

"If I were you," whispered Judy, as they walked along the road towards the tube station, "I should be more careful in future when you pack your suitcase!"

Paddington looked down. A large piece of bacon stuck out of the side of his case and was trailing on the pavement.

"Shoo!" cried Mrs Brown as a grubby-looking dog came bounding across the road. Paddington waved his suitcase. "Go away, dog," he said, sternly. The dog licked its lips and Paddington glanced anxiously over his shoulder as he hurried on, keeping close behind Mrs Brown and Judy.

"Oh dear," said Mrs Brown. "I have a funny feeling about today. As if *things* are going to happen. Do you ever have that feeling, Paddington?"

Paddington considered for a moment. "Sometimes," he said vaguely as they entered the station.

At first Paddington was a little disappointed in the Underground. He liked the noise and the bustle and the smell of warm air which greeted him as they went inside. But he didn't think much of the ticket.

He examined carefully the piece of green cardboard which he held in his paw. "It doesn't seem much to get for tenpence," he said. After all the lovely whirring and clanking noises the ticket machine had made it did seem disappointing. He'd expected much more for his money.

"But Paddington," Mrs Brown sighed, "you only have a ticket so that you can ride on the train. They won't let you on otherwise." She looked and sounded rather flustered. Secretly she was beginning to wish they had waited until later in the day, when it wasn't quite so crowded. There was also the peculiar business of the dogs. Not one, but six dogs of various shapes and sizes had followed them right inside. She had a funny feeling it had something to do with Paddington, but the only time she caught his eye it had such an innocent expression she felt quite upset with herself for having such thoughts.

"I suppose," she said to Paddington, as they stepped on the escalator, "we ought really to carry you. It says you're supposed to carry dogs but it doesn't say anything about bears."

Paddington didn't answer. He was following behind in a dream. Being a very short bear he couldn't easily see over the side, but when he did his eyes nearly popped out with excitement. There were people everywhere. He'd never seen so many. There were people rushing down one side and there were more people rushing up the other. Everyone seemed in a terrible hurry. As he stepped off the escalator he found himself being carried between a man with an umbrella and a lady with a large shopping bag. By the time he managed to push his way free both Mrs Brown and Judy had completely disappeared.

It was then that he saw a most surprising notice. He blinked several times to make sure but each time he opened his eyes it said the same thing: FOLLOW THE AMBER LIGHT TO PADDINGTON.

Paddington decided the Underground was quite the most exciting thing that had ever happened to him. He turned and trotted down the corridor, following the amber lights, until he met another crowd of people who were queuing for the "up" escalator.

"'Ere, 'ere," said the man at the top, as he examined Paddington's ticket. "What's all this? You haven't been anywhere yet!"

"I know," said Paddington, unhappily. "I think I must have made a mistake at the bottom."

The man sniffed suspiciously and called across to an inspector. "There's a young bear 'ere, smelling of bacon. Says he made a mistake at the bottom."

The inspector put his thumbs under his waistcoat. "Escalators is for the benefit and convenience of passengers," he said sternly. "Not for the likes of young bears to play on. Especially in the rush hour."

"Yes, sir," said Paddington, raising his hat. "But we don't have esca . . . esca . . ."

". . . lators," said the inspector, helpfully.

". . . lators," said Paddington, "in Darkest Peru. I've never been on one before, so it's rather difficult."

"Darkest Peru?" said the inspector, looking most impressed. "Oh, well in that case" – he lifted up the chain which divided the "up" and the "down" escalators – "you'd better get back down. But don't let me catch you up to any tricks again."

"Thank you very much," said Paddington gratefully, as he ducked under the chain. "It's very kind of you, I'm sure." He turned to wave goodbye, but before he could raise his hat he found himself being whisked into the depths of the Underground again.

Halfway down he was gazing with interest at the brightly coloured posters on the wall when the man standing behind poked him with his umbrella. "There's someone calling you," he said.

Paddington looked round and was just in time to see Mrs Brown and Judy pass by on their way up. They waved frantically at him and Mrs Brown called out "Stop!" several times.

Paddington turned and tried to run up the escalator, but it was going very fast, and with his short legs it was as much as he could do even to stand still. He had his head down and he didn't notice a fat man with a briefcase who was running in the opposite direction until it was too late.

There was a roar of rage from the fat man and he toppled over and grabbed at several other people. Then Paddington felt himself falling. He went bump, bump, bump all the way down before he shot off the end and finally skidded to a stop by the wall.

When he looked round everything seemed very confused. A number of people were gathered round the fat man, who was sitting on the floor rubbing his head. Away in the distance he could see Mrs Brown and Judy trying to push their way down the "up" escalator. It was while he was watching their efforts that he saw another notice. It was in a brass case at the bottom of the escalator and it said, in big red letters: TO STOP THE ESCALATOR IN CASES OF EMERGENCY PUSH THE BUTTON.

It also said in much smaller letters, "Penalty for Improper Use – £25." But in his

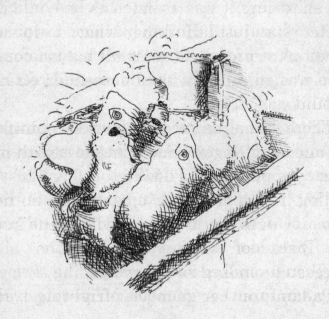

hurry Paddington did not notice this. In any case it seemed to him very much of an emergency. He swung his suitcase through the air and hit the button as hard as he could.

If there had been confusion while the escalator was moving, there was even more when it stopped. Paddington watched with surprise as everyone started running about in different directions shouting at each other. One man even began calling out "Fire!" and somewhere in the distance a bell began to ring.

He was just thinking what a lot of excitement pressing one small button could cause when a heavy hand descended on his shoulder.

"That's him!" someone shouted, pointing an accusing finger. "Saw him do it with me own eyes. As large as life!"

"Hit it with his suitcase," shouted another voice. "Ought not to be allowed!" While from the back of the crowd someone else suggested sending for the police.

Paddington began to feel frightened. He

turned and looked up at the owner of the hand.

"Oh," said a stern voice. "It's *you* again. I might have known." The inspector took out a notebook. "Name, please."

"Er . . . Paddington," said Paddington.

"I said what's your name, not where do you want to go," repeated the inspector.

"That's right," said Paddington. "That *is* my name."

"*Paddington!*" said the inspector, disbelieving. "It can't be. That's the name of a station. I've never heard of a bear called Paddington before."

"It's very unusual," said Paddington. "But it's Paddington Brown, and I live at number thirty-two Windsor Gardens. And I've lost Mrs Brown and Judy."

"Oh!" The inspector wrote something in his book. "Can I see your ticket?"

"Er . . . I had it," said Paddington. "But I don't seem to any more."

The inspector began writing again. "Playing on the escalator. Travelling without a ticket. *Stopping* the escalator. All serious offences they are." He looked up. "What have you got to say to that, young feller me lad?"

"Well . . . er . . ." Paddington shifted uneasily and looked down at his paws.

"Have you tried looking inside your hat?" asked the inspector, not unkindly. "People often put their tickets in there."

Paddington jumped with relief. "I knew I had it somewhere," he said, thankfully, as he handed it to the inspector.

The inspector handed it back again quickly. The inside of Paddington's hat was rather sticky.

"I've never known anyone take so long not to get anywhere," he said, looking at Paddington. "Do you often travel on the Underground?"

"It's the first time," said Paddington.

"And the last if I have anything to do with it," said Mrs Brown as she pushed her way through the crowd.

"Is this your bear, Madam?" asked the inspector. "Because if it is, I have to inform you that he's in serious trouble." He began to read from his notebook. "As far as I can see he's broken two important regulations – probably more. I shall have to give him into custody."

"Oh dear." Mrs Brown clutched at Judy for support. "Do you *have* to? He's only small and it's his first time out in London. I'm sure he won't do it again."

"Ignorance of the law is no excuse," said the inspector, ominously. "Not in court! Persons are expected to abide by the regulations. It says so."

"In court!" Mrs Brown passed a hand nervously over her forehead. The word *court* always upset her. She had visions of Paddington being taken away in handcuffs and being cross-examined and all sorts of awful things.

Judy took hold of Paddington's paw and squeezed it reassuringly. Paddington looked up gratefully. He wasn't at all sure what they were talking about, but none of it sounded very nice.

"Did you say *persons* are expected to abide by the regulations?" Judy asked, firmly.

"That's right," began the inspector. "And I

have my duty to do the same as everyone else."

"But it doesn't say anything about bears?" asked Judy, innocently.

"Well," the inspector scratched his head. "Not in so many words." He looked down at Judy, then at Paddington, and then all around. The escalator had started up again and the crowd of sightseers had disappeared.

"It's all highly irregular," he said, "but . . ."

"Oh, thank you," said Judy. "I think you're the kindest man I've ever met! Don't *you* think so, Paddington?" Paddington nodded his head vigorously and the inspector blushed.

"I shall always travel on this Underground in future," said Paddington, politely. "I'm sure it's the nicest in all London."

The inspector opened his mouth and seemed about to say something, but he closed it again.

"Come along, children," said Mrs Brown, hastily. "If we don't hurry up we shall never get our shopping done."

From somewhere up above came the sound

of some dogs barking. The inspector sighed. "I can't understand it," he said. "This used to be such a well run, respectable station. Now look at it!"

He stared after the retreating figures of Mrs Brown and Judy with Paddington bringing up the rear and then he rubbed his eyes. "That's funny," he said, more to himself. "I must be seeing things. I could have sworn that bear had some bacon sticking out of his case!" He shrugged his shoulders. There were more important things to worry about. Judging by the noise coming from the top of the escalator there was some sort of dog fight going on. It needed investigating.

Julian,
Dream Doctor

Ann Cameron

It was night. My mum was at a meeting. My dad was supposed to have sent us to bed. But one nice thing about him is he usually forgets.

He and Huey and I were sitting on the front porch steps. Above the lawn, fireflies flashed their lights like tiny signalling flying saucers. In the little pine tree by the corner of the house we could hear the soft, thick sounds a bird makes, arranging its wings like blankets, getting ready to sleep.

It was a perfect time to get my dad to talk, a perfect time to find out what to get for his birthday.

"Dad," I said, "what do you love more than anything else in the world?"

My dad stretched his legs out. He smiled.

"You and Huey and Mum."

I was glad he said it. But it was no help in picking a special birthday present. We couldn't give Dad us. He already had us.

"But what do you like more than anything else in the world?" Huey asked. "Deep in your heart," he added.

My dad thought a while.

"I like simple things. For instance – the ocean."

Huey's eyes widened. "That's awfully hard to wrap!" he said.

I kicked Huey's foot.

"What else do you like best of anything?" I asked.

"Something smaller," Huey suggested.

My dad smiled.

"Mountains," he said. "I like mountains, too."

I thought we could wrap a mountain, but I didn't see how we could carry it. Maybe we would ask to have it delivered. The delivery men would have to be very, very big. I imagined them coming to the door. "Package. Special birthday delivery for Ralph Bates," they would say.

"Dad," Huey said, "deep in your heart, what do you really like that's small?"

"Small?" Dad said. "An atom."

"Of course I've never seen one," he added. "But I like the idea of it. I like to think how tiny an atom is, and how much empty space it has inside it, and how many parts it has, all speeding around and knocking into one another like a crazy ride at the fair."

"An atom!" I said. It would not be hard to get. Forks, spoons, tables, dogs, hot dogs, universes and probably even monsters are all made of atoms.

I am made of atoms too. I remembered that and tried shaking one off my hand.

I thought it came loose. Then I tried to pick it up off the step, but I couldn't tell if I had picked it up or not. Maybe I squashed it.

My dad was watching.

"Skeeters biting you, Julian?" he asked.

"A little," I said. I wondered how many

atoms were in a mosquito. Probably about fifteen billion and one. We could give Dad a mosquito for his birthday and make a card that said: "Dear Dad, Here is the atom you asked for, plus fifteen billion extra." But no matter how much Dad liked atoms, I was pretty sure he didn't like skeeters that much.

"How about something . . . not quite so small?" Huey said.

My dad thought a long while.

Huey and I waited. I was sure we were finally going to find it out – Dad's real, catchable, wrappable, deliverable, secret dream.

Dad leaned back. He looked up.

"You know what I really like best of all?" he said. "See way, way up there? That star."

My dad was at his garage. My mum was at her job. Huey was with me.

I was sitting in the back garden, working.

"Suppose Dad doesn't have one?" Huey asked.

"One what?" I said.

"A secret dream," Huey said.

"Dad is a grown-up," I said. "Every grown-up has a secret dream."

I thought I was right, but mostly I said it because I didn't want to give up my great idea.

"If Dad does have a secret dream, how are we going to find it out?" Huey asked.

"It's not going to be easy," I said. "We are going to have to work hard."

"With that stuff?" Huey said. He pointed all around me. I had every one of the big saucepans out in the garden, plus the eggwhisk and the living room fan. I was tying them all together with wire. I had the fan and the eggwhisk tied at the top.

"This is not stuff," I said. "This is equipment."

"What is it going to do?" Huey asked.

"Have you ever heard of brain waves?" I asked.

"No," Huey said.

"Just like there are waves in the ocean, there are invisible waves in the air. That's how radio and TV programmes get to the house – on those waves."

"There aren't little people living in the TV set?" Huey said.

"No," I said, "there aren't." I wired the last pan into the equipment and tied the whole thing to the lowest branch of the big pine tree. I moved Huey so he was directly in front of it.

"Now," I said, "sit here with me."

Huey did.

"Brains also have waves," I said. "With this equipment, we will pick up signals from Dad's brain. If we concentrate on the signal, we will know what he really wants for his birthday."

"Okay," Huey said. He didn't sound convinced.

"Close your eyes," I said. "It helps."

Huey did, and I closed my eyes too.

I concentrated on Dad. On what he wanted, deep in his heart.

We sat a long time. I heard the pans moving in the wind. I heard the fan creak. I did not pick up any brain waves reflected

from the equipment. After a while I heard something fall.

"Did you hear that?" Huey said.

"I did," I said.

"What was it?" Huey said.

"I think it was Mum's stewpan," I said. "Are you getting any messages from Dad?"

"No," Huey said. "But I think I got a message from Mum. About how she doesn't like the pans out on the lawn. Or the fan."

I opened my eyes. I looked at the brain wave receiver.

"Maybe you are right," I said. "Maybe we should take this stuff in."

We put the fan, the eggwhisk and the pans away. I was disappointed.

"It was such a great-looking machine! I can't figure out why it didn't work!" I said. "But never mind. I have another idea."

Huey and I got a rope out of the garage. We took it upstairs. We tied one end to the bedpost of our bed. The other end I tied tight around my waist.

I went to the window. The roof was very close and easy to get to, and it was practically flat. But I liked having the rope. It made me feel like a mountaineer. Also, I don't like taking chances.

I climbed out of the window.

"OK," I said. "Now, Huey, you sit on the bed."

"Why?" Huey said.

"To weigh it down," I said.

"Why?" Huey said.

"In case I fall," I said. "You and the bed will hold me."

"Why would you fall?" Huey said. "The roof is practically flat."

"In case a giant wind comes," I said. "One that could blow me off the roof."

"But there's practically no wind," Huey said.

His questions were spoiling everything.

"Huey," I said, "just sit on the bed."

He did.

I looked around. I felt like an astronaut. "One giant step forward," I said. "For science and for Dad."

I walked slowly like a moonwalker to where the TV aerial was attached to the roof.

I held on to it with both hands.

"Safe!" I shouted. I shut my eyes and thought about Dad. About receiving his message. Using the TV aerial as a receiver, I might see a mental picture of his special present.

The picture would probably be in colour, but I was also ready to receive in black and white.

A long time passed. Huey didn't say anything. Probably he had fallen asleep on the bed.

It was hot. My feet hurt. I got no signal.

Suddenly I heard a man's voice, low, soft and urgent.

It was definitely a TV kind of voice. It sounded like Dad would sound if he was announcing a serious pain remedy.

"Julian," said the voice. "Julian."

It sounded like Dad's brain, waving!

"Receiving," I said softly, "receiving."

"Julian," said the voice, "my truck isn't working . . ."

"Truck broke?" I mentally transmitted. "Birthday present? New truck?"

"So I just jogged home for lunch . . . Julian, this is your father speaking . . ."

I wanted the voice to forget about jogging and get back on the subject.

"I know you're my father," I mentally transmitted. "Birthday present? New truck?"

The volume of the signal went up.

"Julian! Answer me! What are you *doing* tied to your bed, on a rope out of the window, talking to the TV aerial?"

I opened my eyes. I turned around. I let go of the TV aerial. My brain waves shattered.

Dad was staring at me from the window. In colour. In 3-D. Live.

"Dad!" I said. "Happy—" I was going to say happy birthday. But it wasn't his birthday, yet. "Dad!" I said. "Happy day!"

The Missing Nose

David Henry Wilson

Gideon Gander, also known as Gander of the Yard, is certain he is the Greatest Detective in the World – especially after solving the complicated Humpty Dumpty Mystery. Now he is about to set off on another baffling case. How impressed his wife, Mother Goose, will be when he solves it!

"**G**ideon Gander. Come to the Palace immediately. The King wants to see you."

That was the message that started me off on one of my most famous cases. I can't say I was very keen to go back to the Palace. On

my last visit, when I had solved the Humpty Dumpty Mystery, I'd had to dig up a grave, spend hours and hours reading toilet rolls in the Royal Lavatory, fill in the grave, and drag a heavy gravestone with eggcup all the way to the river. And as a reward the King had wished me goodbye and good luck.

"Shall I tell him I can't come?" I asked Mother Goose.

"You can't say 'can't' to a King," she said. "Unless you want your head chopped off."

I decided to take the case.

"It's our maid," said the King. "She's lost her nose, and we've got to find it. If we don't, she won't do any more cooking, washing, cleaning or ironing. It's a national crisis. Find her nose, and there'll be a big reward for you."

The case sounded interesting. So did the reward.

"I'd better see her straight away," I said.

"You can't," said the King. "She's locked herself in the kitchen, and she won't come out till she gets her nose back."

"But I need to know what happened," I said.

"All I can tell you is that she was hanging the clothes out in the garden, screamed, and the next thing we knew was she was locked in the kitchen without her nose."

"I see," I said.

I didn't see, but I had to say something.

"You can talk to her through the kitchen door if you like," said the King. "And by the way, you'd better try to avoid the Queen. She's in a foul temper because she can't get into the kitchen for her food."

The King showed me the way to the kitchen, stopping to peep round every corner in case the Queen was there. She wasn't.

"Probably sulking in the parlour," said the King. "This is the kitchen door."

"Hello, in there!" I called. "Can you hear me?"

"Of course I cad hear you," said a voice. "It's by dose I've lost, dot by ears!"

"This is Superdetective Gideon Gander of the Yard. I'm going to find your nose!"

"Thed what are you doig here? Go add fide it!"

"I need to know what happened," I said.

"I was haggig out the washig id the garded, add suddedly sobthig attacked be add took by dose. That's all I kdow."

"What attacked you?" I asked.

"I dote kdow."

"Think carefully," I said. "Was it a wolf?"

"Do," she said. "If it had beed a wolf, I'd have seed it."

That was a pity. If it wasn't Wolfie, I really didn't have much idea who it could be.

I asked the King to show me the garden where the maid had been hanging out the clothes. Fortunately, I didn't see the Queen, but what I did see when we reached the garden was a whole line of shirts, vests, pants, and fur-lined knickers. They looked suspicious.

"What are these?" I asked.

"Clothes," said the King.

"And what are they doing here?" I asked.

"The maid was hanging them out," said the King.

I quickly formed a theory. The clothes on the line could be the clothes the maid was hanging out when she was attacked. In other words, by sheer chance we were standing on or near the very spot where she had lost her nose.

"It's my belief," I said to the King, "that this is the place where the nose was lost. Let's look for it."

"We have," said the King. "The gardener and I searched every inch of the garden."

"Aha!" I said. "And what did you find?"

"A few flowers," said the King, "and some vegetables, and a lot of weeds."

"Did you find a nose?" I asked.

"Of course we didn't find a nose!" said the King. "If we had, I wouldn't have sent for you!"

His tone was rather rude, but I didn't tell him so. He was probably upset at not having found the nose. Instead, I glanced around the garden and happened to see a black feather lying on the ground. I picked it up.

"Aha!" I said. "What's this?"

"It's a feather," said the King. "And if you ask me any more stupid questions, I shall have your head chopped off."

That was a shock. Rudeness is one thing, but head-chopping is quite another.

"You can't be serious, Your Majesty," I said.

"Just try me," he said.

I needed to impress him quickly. If only I could find a clue! If only I could see the nose!

"Well?" snapped the King. "Can you solve the case or can't you?"

"I think I've solved it already, Your Majesty," I said. I was desperate.

"Where's the nose then?" he asked.

"One step at a time, Your Majesty," I said. "The key to the mystery is . . . is . . . is this feather."

"What about the feather?" he asked.

"You'll soon see," I said.

Then I looked closely at the feather, shook it, listened to it, smelt it, tasted it, held it up in the wind . . .

"Well?" asked the King.

"Well . . ." I said. "Well, well."

"Well what?"

"Well, well, well."

"What have you found out?" he asked.

"Do you notice anything special about this feather, Your Majesty?" I asked him.

"No," he said.

That was a pity. I'd hoped he would. I certainly hadn't.

"Except that it's black," he said.

"Aha!" I said. "Precisely! And what does that mean?"

"I suppose it's fallen off a black bird."

That was good thinking. It might even be a clue, though I still didn't see what it had to do with the missing nose.

"Exactly," I said. "A black bird. The vital clue."

"So where's the nose?" asked the King.

"Just a few more questions, Your Majesty,"

I said, "and all will be revealed."

I was in terrible trouble. If all wasn't revealed, then as far as I was concerned, all would be over. My only hope was to keep asking questions. Maybe the King would get tired, or hungry, or bored, and go away. Maybe the Queen would come and drag him off to the parlour.

"Where were you, Your Majesty, at the moment of the crime?"

"In the counting house," said the King.

"And where was the Queen?" I asked.

"In the parlour, eating bread and honey."

"And where was the gardener?"

"Washing up after lunch."

"And what did you have for lunch?"

"Blackbird pie."

"And what was in the blackbird pie?"

"Blackbirds, you silly goo . . . ah! Wait a moment!"

For some reason the King held up his hand. There was a look on his face which in a strange way reminded me of the dawn.

"Wait a moment!" he said again.

I waited. I was prepared to wait an hour so

81

long as he didn't chop off my head.

"Blackbird pie . . ." he said. "Made with a pocketful of rye and twenty-four blackbirds. A very dainty dish it was, too. But I see what you're getting at."

I was glad he did. I certainly didn't.

"In fact," he said, "something very interesting happened after we'd opened the pie."

"What was that, Your Majesty?" I asked.

"The birds began to sing," he said.

"The twenty-four blackbirds?" I asked.

"No," he said. "They'd been baked. It was the birds in the garden – they made a terrible din."

"That's very interesting," I said.

Actually, I thought it was rather boring, but you don't tell a King he's boring. Unless you want to lose your head.

"I remember thinking at the time," said the King, "that it was a protest. Blackbirds protesting about unfair treatment to blackbirds. It happens all the time. Usually it's people protesting about unfair treatment to people. It's a rotten life being a King.

Everybody's always protesting about something. That's why I spend so much time in the counting house – it's the only place where I can get any peace."

"Tsk, tsk," I said. "Poor you."

"Well, this theory of yours could be right," said the King.

"What theory's that?" I asked.

"That a blackbird took the maid's nose as a protest."

"Exactly!" I said. "The blackbird did it!"

I didn't quite see how I'd reached that conclusion, but if the King thought I was right, then so did I.

"The problem is," said the King, "how do we get the nose back?"

He looked at me as though he expected an answer. I though that was a bit unfair, since I didn't even know how the nose had been lost in the first place. But I remembered something my old mother had told me when I was just a tiny gosling:

"Maybe if you asked nicely . . ." I said.

"That's it!" cried the King. "I'll ask them to give it back, and I'll promise never to eat blackbird pie again."

"What a good idea, Your Majesty!" I said.

If he was happy with it, I was happy with it.

He hurried off to the counting house, and came back with a large sheet of paper and a pencil. Then, very slowly and carefully, he wrote out the following message:

PLEASE CAN WE HAVE OUR MAID'S
NOSE BACK
AND WE'LL NEVER EAT ANOTHER
BIRD THAT'S BLACK
signed, The King

Then he stuck it up on the Palace wall, and we waited.

We'd hardly waited for one minute when there was a flutter of black and a swoosh of pink, and there in front of us on the garden path lay a nose.

"We've done it!" cried the King. "We've got the nose back! Congratulations, Goose, my boy, you've saved the kingdom! I shall give you a knighthood for this. Wait here. I'll be back in a minute."

He rushed off, holding the nose, and I waited in the garden feeling rather pleased with myself. Mother Goose would have quite a surprise when she learned she was now married to Sir Gideon Gander. And it would be a shock for Wolfie, too. He'd have to show a bit more respect for me now that I was a knight. Maybe I'd have some visiting cards printed: *Sir Gideon Gander, Superdetective.* Then the whole town would know.

The King came back.

"Here you are, Goose," he said. "This is

your reward, and well done again!"

He handed me a small piece of black cloth.

"Thank you, Your Majesty," I said. "What is it?"

"It's a nighthood," said the King. "You slip it over your head at night. Shuts out all the light and the noise, so you'll sleep better. The King of France gave it to me, but I couldn't breathe with it on, so you can have it. Goodbye, Goose, and good luck."

It wasn't the reward I'd expected, but when I showed it to Mother Goose, she said it was better to have a hood for my head than no head at all. And I could still tell everyone that the King had given me a knighthood, if I wanted to.

That night, I put the hood over my head and very nearly suffocated. I couldn't breathe with it on. If Mother Goose hadn't taken it off me in time, it would have been another case for investigation. But Sir Gideon Gander, Superdetective, would not have been there to solve it.

Emily's Legs

Dick King-Smith

To begin with, nobody noticed.

Mind you, you couldn't blame Mother Spider. If she'd only had one baby, she'd have been sure to notice.

But she had a hundred babies, all hatching out at the same time. How could she be expected to know that ninety-nine spiderlings were normal and one was different?

Father Spider didn't notice. For one thing, he didn't like children.

For another, he was always too busy sitting quite still, waiting for houseflies and bluebottles to land in his web, in the highest darkest corner of the room.

Emily's ninety-nine brothers and sisters didn't notice.

Nobody noticed, not even Emily, until the night of the Spider Sports.

For the grown-up spiders, there were lots of different events. There was web-spinning (how quickly could you make a whole one from start to finish) and fly-parcelling (how quickly could you tie up a fly in silken threads) and fly-eating (how quickly could you . . . yes, well, I needn't explain that).

And there was abseiling, where you let out a thread and whizzed down it from the ceiling, and thread-climbing, where you whizzed back up again.

But for the spiderlings there were only the eight-legged races.

Now this was where Emily's troubles began.

Not that she didn't run in the eight-legged races at the Spider Sports.

She did.

Not that she didn't win.

She did.

The trouble was that she won them all and she won them all so easily.

First, all the spiderlings were lined up at one end of the room, and they had to race across the carpet to the other end.

Emily won easily.

Then they had to race up the wall of the room.

Emily won easily.

Then they had to race down the wall.

Emily won easily.

Last of all was the upside-down eight-legged race, right across the ceiling.

Yes, you've guessed, Emily won easily.

"Amazing!" said all the grown-up spiders. "Well done, Emily!"

But the spiderlings weren't so happy.

"Why does Emily *always* win?" they asked one another.

"Why does Emily *always* win?" they asked the grown-up spiders.

"Because she's the fastest, of course," said the grown-up spiders in the knowing way that old folk have.

"But *why* is she the fastest?" asked the spiderlings in the annoying way that young folk have. And that was when the truth was discovered.

Emily was asked to appear in front of the

Spider Sports Committee to receive her prizes, four neatly parcelled little flies.

"Congratulations, Emily," said the chair-person of the Sports Committee. "You have won all four eight-legged races. Why is that, do you think?"

"If you please," said Emily (for she was by nature a polite spiderling), "it's because I ran the fastest."

"Ah!" said a very old grown-up spider. "But *why* did you run the fastest?"

Emily scratched her head with her two front legs. "I don't really know," she said modestly. "I suppose I just legged it quicker than they did."

"Legged it?" said the very old grown-up spider.

"Legged it?" said all the other grown-up spiders.

And they all looked carefully at Emily's legs.

They weren't any different from the legs of all the other spiderlings. They were no longer. They were no stronger. They were no hairier. But suddenly they all saw that, though Emily was scratching her head with her two front legs, yet she was still standing on eight others.

Emily had ten legs!

For a moment nobody spoke.

Then, "Disgraceful!" said the very old grown-up spider.

"Disgusting!" cried the chairperson of the Sports Committee.

"Disqualified!" shouted all the other grown-up spiders.

Then Emily was made to hand back the four neatly parcelled fly-prizes, and the Committee scuttled off to spread the news.

When Mother Spider heard it, she went straight up the wall.

"Egbert!" she shouted. "Egbert!" (for that was Father Spider's name). "Where are you?"

Father Spider was where he always was, in the highest darkest corner of the room.

At first he did not answer. His wife sounded angry. Like most of his kind, he was a good deal smaller than she was. A number of his old friends had disappeared, suddenly and completely, on account of their wives being angry.

Or hungry.

Or both.

He tensed himself for a quick getaway, and as he saw his large wife approaching, he called out in a syrupy voice, "Why, Muriel," (for that was Mother Spider's name), "whatever is the matter, dearest?"

"Oh Egbert!" cried Mother Spider. "It's Emily!"

"Who is Emily?"

"One of our children. Oh, the little wretch! Oh the shame! Oh, I'm so embarrassed!"

"Why?"

"She has ten legs," said Mother Spider in a horrified voice.

Now as soon as Father Spider was sure that his wife was not angry with *him*, he changed his tune completely.

"Look here, Muriel," he said sternly. "First of all, you know that I don't like children. Second, I couldn't care less how many legs they have – she's lucky, this Emily, she's got a couple of spares. And third, I object to being interrupted when I'm busy."

"But you're not doing anything."

"Yes, I am. I'm busy sitting still, waiting for houseflies and bluebottles. Kindly go away!"

Meanwhile Emily sat silent, alone with her thoughts. She had counted her legs carefully, first clockwise, then anticlockwise, but the answer came out the same either way – ten.

Emily felt sad, as anyone would who had been disqualified and had her prizes taken away and been shouted at by a Sports Committee.

And Mother and Father will be angry too,

I suppose, she thought. Grown-ups! They're all the same.

Then she cheered up a bit. At least my brothers and sisters won't care, she thought. I'll go down to the Gym and have some fun. And off she scuttled (very fast, of course).

The Gym was an old dusty cupboard where the spiderlings gathered to practise making their first very small webs, and to do abseiling and climbing and generally enjoy themselves. A number of large disused webs hung across the cupboard, and these acted as safety nets for those who fell by mistake, and trampolines for those who fell on purpose.

Ten or a dozen spiderlings were in the Gym when Emily arrived, but the moment they saw her, they all stopped doing whatever they were doing and stared at her in silence.

Then one of them spoke.

"Cheat!" it said in a nasty voice. "You're a cheat!"

And then the rest joined in.

"Who's a clever girl then?"

"Won all the races!"

"The eight-legged races!"

"But she's got ten legs!"

"Cheat! Cheat! Dirty cheat!"

"I didn't know," Emily said. "Honest, I didn't know I had ten." But they went on yelling, which made her angry.

"Anyway," she said, "I bet I could beat you lot with two legs tied behind my back."

At this, there was once again silence in the Gym. Then the first spiderling spoke again in a voice that was even nastier.

"You're never going to be given the chance," it said. "Come on, everybody. Get her!"

Emily ran out of the Gym as fast as her ten legs would carry her. She ran down the wall, dashed across the carpet, and hid in a crack in the skirting board. She waited, facing outwards. The crack was narrow, so that they would only be able to come at her one at a time.

"I'll jolly well show 'em," she said to herself. "Calling me a cheat. They'd better be careful."

She could hear the spiderlings chattering

to each other as they ran about the room in search of her.

"Wait till we find her!"

"We'll make her wish she'd never been hatched!"

"We'll show her!"

"We'll show Miss Emily Ten-legs!"

"Let's pull off one of them!"

"Let's pull off two! Then she'd be a proper spider!"

You just try it, thought Emily. I'm not afraid of you.

But she was, and it was a great relief to hear her mother's voice, calling angrily to the others.

"What are you doing, you naughty children?" she cried to the gang of spiderlings.

"Just playing," they said.

"How many times have I told you not to play out in the room in broad daylight? Stay in the Gym, or under the chairs, or behind the curtains," said Mother Spider.

Then she used the threat that mother spiders everywhere use to frighten their naughty children.

"If you're not careful," she said, "the Hoover will get you! Now scuttle off, the lot of you!"

Emily waited till the spiderlings had gone, and then she came out of her hole. I'd better face the music, she thought. She can't eat me, after all. Or can she?

"Mother?" she said, a little nervously.

Mother Spider was hanging from the lampshade. She let out thread rapidly and came whizzing down to the floor. She did not look best pleased. Emily crossed two of her legs for luck.

Mother Spider walked all round her slowly. As she went, she counted out loud.

"So it's true," she said at last in a low voice. "It's true what they're saying. Never have I been so embarrassed."

'I didn't know, Mother," said Emily. "Honest, I didn't know I had ten."

"Nor did I," said Mother Spider. "But now that I do, I've only one thing to say to you."

"What's that?"

"Never darken my web again!" said Mother Spider, and she reeled in thread and shot up into the lampshade without a backward look.

Emily sighed.

Perhaps my father will be kinder, she thought. She had never met him, but she knew where he lived.

She ran round the edge of the room, keeping a sharp eye out for other spiderlings, and began to climb up to the highest darkest corner.

Father Spider was busy sitting still when he felt a slight shudder on his web. He dashed out, to find, not a housefly or a bluebottle, but a spiderling.

"Father?" said Emily, a little nervously.

"Go away!" said Father Spider crossly. "You know I don't like children."

"But I'm your daughter."

"I have hundreds of daughters," said Father Spider, "and hundreds of sons, and I don't like any of them."

"But I'm Emily."

"The one with ten legs?"

"Yes," said Emily. "I didn't know, Father," she said. "Honest, I didn't know I had ten."

"What are you moaning about?" said Father Spider. "Think yourself lucky. You've got a couple of spares."

He pulled back the thread on which Emily was standing.

"Get lost!" he said, and he let it go with a twang.

Emily was hurled from the web like a stone from a catapult.

At the same time the room was filled with a sudden roaring noise that grew louder as Emily fell until, as she hit the floor, it was very loud indeed.

And very close.

Dazed and helpless, Emily could only watch as the monster rushed towards her.

Her mother's words echoed in her brain.

"The Hoover will get you!"

In time to come, when Emily was herself a mother spider, her own spiderlings often asked her for a web-time story. And their favourite was "The Day The Hoover Ate Mum." They knew, because they had heard it so often, that it had a happy ending.

But a happy ending was the last thing Emily expected when she was sucked into the mouth of the vacuum cleaner.

The first thing she felt was a sharp pain (two sharp pains, to be exact).

Then she found herself in a thick choking blackness, unable to see or to cry out – for her eyes and mouth were full of dust – and unable to hear anything but the dreadful deafening noise of the machine. For a moment, Emily thought she was dead.

But then the Hoover was switched off, the heap of fluff and dirt settled to the bottom of the bag, and Emily fought her way to the top of it.

To her surprise and relief she found she was not alone, for suddenly a voice rang out in the darkness.

"All clear, my lads!" it cried. "Us can unroll now."

Once her eyes had grown accustomed to the darkness, Emily could see that the speaker was a large woodlouse, and that several other woodlice had climbed to the top of the pile of dust. They looked at Emily in a friendly manner.

"Hello, young 'un," said the first woodlouse. "You'm looking a bit gloomy."

"I am," said Emily. "Nobody likes me. Not my mother nor my father nor my horrid brothers and sisters."

"Whyever not?"

"Because I've got ten legs."

"Poor little mite!" cried the woodlouse. "Only ten!"

"Why do you say 'only' ten?" said Emily.

"Because you should have fourteen by rights. All woodlice has fourteen legs."

"But she's not a woodlouse," said a voice behind Emily. "She's a spider."

Emily turned round to see a spiderling, a little smaller than herself, emerging from the dust-pile.

"Who are you?" she said.

"My name's James," said the spiderling. "What's yours?"

"Emily," said Emily. "I hope you're not one of my brothers?"

"I hope not," said James. "They don't sound very nice."

"They're not," said Emily. "They're horrible to me. And so are my sisters. And so are my mother and father."

"What are your parents' names?" said James.

"Muriel and Egbert."

"Never heard of them."

"Good. Then you can't be related to me."

"No," said James. "But when we get out of here, I'd like to be." And he put one of his legs round Emily's waist.

"Oh, don't be so soppy," cried Emily, pushing him away. "Anyway, we're never going to get out of here."

"Oh yes you will, young 'un!" cried the woodlice.

"All you got to do is wait . . ."

". . . till they empties the Hoover bag . . ."

". . . into the dustbin . . ."

". . . and then you climbs up the inside of it . . ."

". . . and the next time they do take the lid off . . ."

". . . out you pops!"

"But when will they empty it?" said Emily.

"Soon, I should think," said James. "It's pretty full," and hardly were the words out of his mouth when they all felt the Hoover being lifted, and carried away, and set down again.

Then they heard the zip of the outer cover being undone, and the thick paper bag in which they were all imprisoned shook.

"Watch out, my lads!" shouted the first woodlouse. "We'm a-going!"

"Quickly, Emily," said James. "Attach safety-lines!"

He was only just in time, because at that moment the bottom of the paper bag was opened, and dirt and dust and fluff and woodlice fell into the dustbin.

The bag was empty, save for the two spiderlings suspended within it; and before it could be closed again Emily and James let out thread, swung themselves to the side of the dustbin, and scampered up the wall of it and over the rim and away.

They scuttled for the nearest cover and crouched there breathlessly till all was quiet again.

Then James began to stare at Emily's legs.

Next, he walked all around her slowly. As he went, he counted out loud.

"Oh, don't *you* start!" cried Emily. "If you don't like me having ten legs, you can jolly well push off!"

James stopped at the count of eight.

"You haven't," he said.

"Haven't what?"

"Haven't got ten legs. You've got eight.

104

Same as any other spider."

And then Emily remembered the sharp pain (two sharp pains, to be exact) as the Hoover had sucked her in.

"Except you're not the same as any other spider, Emily," said James. "You're prettier. I think it would be nice if we set up web together," and once again he put one of his legs round Emily's waist.

"Oh don't be so soppy!" cried Emily. But this time she did not push him away.

"And anyway," said James, "they'll grow again."

"What will?"

"The two legs you lost. Spiders of our sort can do that."

"How d'you know?"

"My dad's done it. Mum lost her temper with him one day and pulled off one of his, and he grew a lovely new one."

"Gosh!" said Emily excitedly. "Then I'll still be the fastest spider of them all!"

"Yes."

"But oh!" said Emily miserably. "You won't like me any more, James. Not with ten legs."

"Emily," said James. "When legs are as beautiful as yours, you cannot possibly have too many of them." And he stroked one of hers with one of his.

"Oh James!" said Emily happily. "You say the soppiest things!"

The Stowaways

Roger McGough

When I lived in Liverpool, my best friend was a boy called Midge. Kevin Midgeley was his real name, but we called him Midge for short. And he was short, only about three cornflake packets high (empty ones at that). No three ways about it. Midge was my best friend and we had lots of things in common. Things we enjoyed doing like . . . climbing trees, playing footy, going to the pictures, hitting each other really hard. And there were things we didn't enjoy doing like . . . sums, washing behind our ears, eating cabbage.

But there was one thing that really bound us together, one thing we had in common – a love of the sea.

In the old days (but not so long ago) the River Mersey was far busier than it is today. Those were the days of the great passenger liners and cargo boats. Large ships sailed out of Liverpool for Canada, the United States, South Africa, the West Indies, all over the world. My father had been to sea and so had all my uncles, and my grandfather. Six foot six, muscles rippling in the wind, huge hands grappling with the helm, rum-soaked and fierce as a wounded shark (and that was only my grandmother!) By the time they were twenty, most young men in this city had visited parts of the globe I can't even spell.

In my bedroom each night, I used to lie in bed (best place to lie really), I used to lie there, especially in winter, and listen to the foghorns being sounded all down the river. I could picture the ship nosing its way out of the docks into the channel and out into the Irish Sea. It was exciting. All those exotic places. All those exciting adventures.

Midge and I knew what we wanted to do when we left school . . . become sailors. A captain, an admiral, perhaps one day even a steward. Of course we were only about seven or eight at the time so we thought we'd have a long time to wait. But oddly enough, the call of the sea came sooner than we'd expected.

It was a Wednesday if I remember rightly. I never liked Wednesdays for some reason. I could never spell it for a start and it always seemed to be raining, and there were still two days to go before the weekend. Anyway, Midge and I got into trouble at school. I don't remember what for (something trivial I suppose like chewing gum in class, forgetting

how to read, setting fire to the music teacher), I forget now. But we were picked on, nagged, told off and all those boring things that grown-ups get up to sometimes.

And, of course, to make matters worse, my mum and dad were in a right mood when I got home. Nothing to do with me, of course, because as you have no doubt gathered by now, I was the perfect child: clean, well-mannered, obedient . . . soft in the head. But for some reason I was clipped round the ear and sent to bed early for being childish. Childish! I ask you. I *was* a child. A child acts his age, what does he get? Wallop!

So that night in bed, I decided . . . Yes, you've guessed it. I could hear the big ships calling out to each other as they sidled out of the Mersey into the oceans beyond. The tugs leading the way like proud little guide dogs. That's it. We'd run away to sea, Midge and I. I'd tell him the good news in the morning.

The next two days just couldn't pass quickly enough for us. We had decided to begin our amazing around-the-world voyage on Saturday morning so that in case we didn't like it we would be back in time for school on Monday. As you can imagine there was a lot to think about – what clothes to take, how much food and drink. We decided on two sweaters each and wellies in case we ran into storms around Cape Horn. I read somewhere that sailors lived off rum and dry biscuits, so I poured some of my dad's into an empty pop bottle, and borrowed a handful of half-coated chocolate digestives. I also packed my lonestar cap gun and Midge settled on a magnifying glass.

On Friday night we met round at his house to make the final plans. He lived with his granny and his sister, so there were no nosy parents to discover what we were up to. We hid all the stuff in the shed in the yard and arranged to meet outside his back door next morning at the crack of dawn, or sunrise – whichever came first.

Sure enough, Saturday morning, when the big finger was on twelve and the little one was on six, Midge and I met with our little bundles under our arms and ran up the street as fast as our tiptoes could carry us.

Hardly anyone was about, and the streets were so quiet and deserted except for a few pigeons straddling home after all-night parties. It was a very strange feeling, as if we were the only people alive and the city belonged entirely to us. And soon the world would be ours as well – once we'd stowed away on a ship bound for somewhere far off and exciting.

By the time we'd got down to the Pier Head, though, a lot more people were up and about, including a policeman who eyed us suspiciously. "Ello, ello, ello," he said, "and where are you two going so early in the morning?"

"Fishing," I said.

"Train spotting," said Midge and we looked at each other.

"Just so long as you're not running away to sea."

"Oh no," we chorused. "Just as if."

He winked at us. "Off you go then, and remember to look both ways before crossing your eyes."

We ran off and straight down on to the landing stage where a lot of ships were tied up. There was no time to lose because already quite a few were putting out to sea, their sirens blowing, the hundreds of sea-gulls squeaking excitedly, all tossed into the air like giant handfuls of confetti.

Then I noticed a small ship just to the left where the crew were getting ready to cast off. They were so busy doing their work that it was easy for Midge and me to slip on board unnoticed. Up the gangplank we went and straight up on to the top deck where there was nobody around. The sailors were all too busy down below, hauling in the heavy ropes and revving up the engine that turned the great propellers.

We looked around for somewhere to hide. "I know, let's climb down the funnel," said Midge.

"Great idea," I said, taking the mickey. "Or better still, let's disguise ourselves as a pair of seagulls and perch up there on the mast."

Then I spotted them. The lifeboats. "Quick, let's climb into one of those, they'll never look in there – not unless we run into icebergs anyway." So in we climbed, and no sooner had we covered ourselves with the tarpaulin than there was a great shuddering and the whole ship seemed to turn round on itself. We were off! Soon we'd be digging for diamonds in the Brazilian jungle or building sandcastles on a tropical island. But we had to be patient, we knew that. Those places are a long way away, it could take days, even months.

So we were patient. Very patient. Until after what seemed like hours and hours we decided to eat our rations, which I divided up equally. I gave Midge all the rum and I had all the biscuits. Looking back on it now, that probably wasn't a good idea, especially for Midge.

What with the rolling of the ship, and not having had any breakfast, and the excitement, and a couple of swigs of rum – well, you can guess what happened – woooorrppp! All over the place. We pulled back the sheet and decided to give ourselves up. We were too far away at sea now for the captain to turn back. The worst he could do was to clap us in irons or shiver our timbers.

We climbed down on to the deck and as Midge staggered to the nearest rail to feed the fishes, I looked out to sea hoping to catch sight of a whale, a shoal of dolphins, perhaps see the coast of America coming into view. And what did I see? The Liver Buildings.

Anyone can make a mistake, can't they? I mean we weren't to know we'd stowed away on a ferryboat.

One that goes from Liverpool to Birkenhead and back again, toing and froing across the Mersey. We'd done four trips hidden in the lifeboat and ended up back in Liverpool. And we'd only been away about an hour and a half. "Ah, well, so much for running away to sea," we thought as we disembarked (although disembowelled might be a better word as far as Midge was concerned). Rum? Yuck.

We got the bus home. My mum and dad were having their breakfast. "Aye, aye," said my dad, "here comes the earlybird. And what have you been up to then?"

"I ran away to sea," I said.

"Mm, that's nice," said my mum, shaking out the cornflakes. "That's nice."

The Worm Hunt

Diana Hendry

Jess, Ned and their mum live in a rambling old house. Kid Kibble is to be their eighth lodger. The previous seven have all been disasters! But Kid looks like being the most amazing one yet – and he's Jess and Ned's teacher!

Kid Kibble had a skeleton hung over his left shoulder, three mice cages slung round his waist, a trombone over his right shoulder and a clutch of plastic bags in his one free hand.

"You don't mind Ernest, do you?" Kid Kibble asked, nodding at the skeleton. "He comes everywhere with me. I'd never have passed my exams without him."

"Well, no . . ." said Mum, whose life must be ruined by politeness. "I suppose he's been dead a long time?" (You could tell she was thinking that Ernest might clip-clop out of the attic one night on his bony feet.)

"Oh, at least three centuries!" laughed Kid Kibble, and he and Ernest rattled up to the attic. Rattled is the right word because apart from the three cages, there seemed to be a lot of rattly objects in Kid Kibble's luggage. He paused at the top of the stairs. "Don't mind me," he called down. "It's just my big game traps."

Mum gave her small polite laugh as if she were quite used to having lodgers who went big game hunting after school. We all went into the kitchen while Kid Kibble unpacked. Jess sat at the table and added another question to the questionnaire. It read, "Do you travel with a skeleton?"

"Biology equipment," said Mum, making herself a cup of tea. "That's what it will be. Biology equipment for school. Things for teaching with."

At that moment there was a terrific wail

from the attic as though someone had caught their fingers in the door. We made for the stairs with Jess in the lead.

There, in the middle of the attic, stood Kid Kibble, trombone to his lips, blasting "Rhapsody in Blue" into Ernest's dumb skull.

"Just trying it out," said Kid Kibble giving us all his Hallowe'en turnip grin and shaking trombone spit on to the carpet. "Does anyone else play? We could make a band."

"I play the violin," I said. "But just Grade Two."

"Great!" said Kid Kibble. (I noticed he'd already knocked a nail into the beam and hung Ernest from it.) "We'll have a jam session."

"Don't get too friendly," Jess whispered as we went downstairs. "A teacher's a teacher, not a human being. You can smell them!"

"He wears jeans," I said. Jeans, in my opinion, are like chips and dogs. A person who likes all three is likely to be very liveable with.

"That's just a disguise," said Jess darkly.

*

As it happened, it was rather difficult *not* being friendly with Kid Kibble. After lunch he said, "Fancy some big game hunting?"

Now I don't think Poops, Loopey and Dash have ever heard the words "big game hunting" in all their doggy lives, but they seemed to know it. They were there in a flash, Poops and Loopey sitting at his feet, thumping their tails and gazing up at him, while Dash ran round in excited circles.

"What are you going to hunt?" I asked. Kid Kibble was such an oddball that I half thought he might know of some ancient swamp where prehistoric monsters still lurked. Perhaps he was planning to bring the last dinosaur to a biology class. Jess gave me a don't-get-friendly kick under the table.

"Worms," said Kid Kibble, making them sound as fierce as tigers. "I'm going on a worm hunt so I can dissect them with the second years."

"I'm sorry," said Jess primly, "but we're both going out to lunch, aren't we, Ned?"

"What a pity," said Kid Kibble. "I wanted

someone to pretend to be rain."

I couldn't stop myself asking what he wanted *that* for, even though Jess was making my ankles black and blue.

"Well, it's what birds do to get the worms out," said Kid Kibble. "They tap the ground with their feet imitating raindrops and the worms hear them and pop up."

I looked at Jess. I badly wanted to go worm hunting. Calling worms up out of the ground reminded me of Indian snake charmers – perhaps that's what they did on their drums, drummed large boomy raindrops. I thought Kid would know if I got the right moment to ask him. Jess shrugged as if to say, "do-what-you-like-but-I'll-get-you-later."

"Perhaps I could come after all," I said, "and pretend to be rain."

"Let's see your fingers," said Kid. I spread them out on the table. "Oh yes," he said. "Quite good for rain."

Jess snorted. "Oh, Sir!" she jeered. "You do have winning ways!"

"Jess!" said Mum. Kid said nothing. He went off to the attic to fetch jamjars for the worm hunt. (I think Kid told all his secret troubles to Ernest.)

We went down to the fields taking Poops, Loopey and Dash with us. Kid certainly liked dogs. I wondered if this might give him a good mark in Jess's books. We squatted down in a shady corner on the edge of the field.

It was full of bluebells. And worms!

Kid marked out a square and I drummed very lightly on the earth, pretending to be rain. Those worms came up one after the other, oozing up from their underworld, fat and thin worms, straight and wiggly worms, all soft and boneless and undressed-looking, as if once upon a time they might have had nice long shells. Kid filched them out of the soil and dropped them into a jamjar. It was like watching a conjuring trick.

"Why do they come out for rain?" I asked. "Do they want a drink?"

Kid laughed. "No, no," he said, "they think they're going to be flooded out down there."

Poops, Loopey and Dash weren't at all interested in worm hunting. They ran about hunting strange smells that made all three of them quiver with excitement.

When we'd got a jamjar full of worms we sat with our backs against a tree and Kid produced a bar of chocolate from his knapsack. I knew he was worried about his first lessons in the morning because every now and then he'd get out a book called *The Craft of the Classroom: A Survival Guide*. He'd look at a page and sigh and put it away again.

"The trouble is," said Kid, "that it's not so long since I was at school myself. I don't really look like a teacher, do I?"

"Well," I said, not wanting to discourage him, "if you wore a tie and flattened your hair down a bit . . ." There was a shoot of hair just about dead centre of Kid Kibble's head that seemed determined to stand up and wave to the world.

We finished the chocolate and walked home. Kid had packed lots of soil into the jars of worms and they'd wriggled down inside it.

Jess was really bad tempered when we got

home. She had a line in Black Looks. When Jess gave you a Black Look you just withered into the earth like a worm going down. She was giving them all to Kid Kibble that day. And you could tell that although he was trying not to wither, he was feeling smaller and smaller by the minute. Jess kept calling him "Sir" in a nasty sort of way. "Have some bread and butter . . . *Sir*?" or "Sugar in your tea . . . *Sir*?" It was the pause before the "sir" that did it, made it sound as if she was really saying, "Sugar in your tea . . . *Slug*?"

"I think you can keep the 'sir' for school and call Kid 'Kid' at home," said Mum at last and at that Jess got up from the table and went out of the kitchen banging the door behind her.

I found her out in the garden, slumped in a deckchair with a hat over her eyes.

"He's not that bad," I said.

"He's awful!" said Jess from under the hat. "He's good and clean. I hate people like that."

"You like them b-b-b-bad and d-d-d-dirty, I suppose?" I said. (The stutter came because I realized suddenly that I wanted Jess and Kid to like each other.)

"Yes, I do!" shouted Jess. "I do! I do! I do!" And she threw off the hat to give me a treble Black Look. I shrugged and began to walk away. "And I'll get him too!" shouted Jess after me. "You just wait and see!"

I didn't have long to wait. About midnight there was a terrible scream from Mum. When I ran out of my bedroom I saw her standing at the top of the stairs clutching her nightie. Her feet seemed glued to the carpet.

"Worms!" she said in a very small and shaky voice. "Worms everywhere!"

Well, that wasn't quite true. They weren't *everywhere*. But there did seem to be at least six, and the fattest six – unless they'd grown since Kid and I collected them. They were wriggling about the carpet as if wondering why it wasn't grass and one of them seemed on the point of exploring Mum's petrified toes.

I ran for a box and picked up the worms. They were twitching in the light. Mum unstuck her feet.

"Biology!" she said bitterly, and not for the last time. "Why can't he teach geography or history or something nice, like art?"

She put on her dressing gown then and we marched up to Kid Kibble's attic, Mum looking very haughty and cross, and me, like the Queen's attendant, carrying the box of worms.

Mum rattled the latch of Kid's door. I could tell from her face that on the way upstairs she'd prepared a long speech all about lodgers not being allowed worms or girlfriends in their rooms after midnight, but it fell from her when we went in and saw Kid Kibble on his hands and knees under the bed, with a torch in one hand and a ruler in the other, searching for worms. The bedclothes had been thrown back. The remains of the soil and one or two worms still wriggled on the bottom sheet. Kid came out, bottom first, a long worm held between finger and thumb.

Mum stepped back a pace. Ernest, in the draught from the open door, shook his bones like wind chimes.

"I really am very sorry," said Kid Kibble. "I don't know how these worms got out of the jars . . ."

But *we* knew, Mum and I.

"Jess!" said Mum. "And I'm the one to be sorry."

"A sort of practical joke, I suppose," said

Kid with a half-Hallowe'en grin. "Not an apple-pie bed. A worm-squirming bed."

"Not a very funny joke," said Mum.

But I had the giggles by then and Kid caught them and eventually Mum stopped looking cross and began to giggle too.

"I'll go and get you a clean sheet," she said.

Kid and I crawled about the attic looking for worms and popping them back into the jamjars. Kid had to go out into the garden in his pyjamas and get some more soil.

Just when we'd screwed the lids on the jars I found one more worm about to wriggle into Kid's slipper and a big fat one curled up on *The Craft of the Classroom* which you couldn't see because the cover of the book was worm-colour.

Then we made Kid's bed again and we all went to sleep although it was about two weeks before anyone felt like walking about upstairs in bare feet.

And that was just the first thing that went wrong for Kid Kibble.

Florizella and
the Giant

Philippa Gregory

*News of an enormous giant arrives at the
kingdom ruled by Princess Florizella's
parents. Somehow the king must get rid of
him. Anxious to find the giant first, practical
and resourceful Florizella sets out with her
friend Prince Bennett. But Simon turns out to
be a gentle giant with a very unfortunate
problem . . .*

The king and queen, who had taken a
good long time to get the royal court
moving, were actually only an hour away
from the giant when Florizella and Bennett
met them on the road. With the royal

procession was the royal zoo keeper, the royal surveyor, the royal enchanter, two hundred of the royal guard and about a hundred other people who had nothing better to do on a fine summer's day than to come along and see what was happening.

"Hullo Florizella!" the king said, as Florizella came cantering up on Jellybean. "Found the giant?"

"Yes!" Florizella said in a rush. "He's only young and he's short-sighted and lonely. But he *will* go back to his own country if we can help him plant his vegetable garden."

The king blinked a bit. "Oh good," he said. He smiled at the queen. "Looks like Florizella has it all under control," he said. "Perhaps we should go home and leave it all to her."

The queen smiled. "I'll just see this giant before we go," she said. "Sometimes Florizella's ideas get a little out of hand."

"How do you make spectacles?" Florizella interrupted.

"I expect I could magic a little something," the royal enchanter offered grandly.

"Go on then," Florizella said.

There was a small clap of thunder and a puff of green smoke and in the road before them stood the most amazing scene. There were dancing girls with ostrich feathers in their hair, there were elephants, there were fireworks exploding brightly in the sky, there were trapeze artists, there was a railway train painted in gold with a song-and-dance ragtime band on silver wagons behind it, there were dancing bears, there were acrobats, there were jugglers, there were fountains pouring into silver basins, there were rose petals tumbling down in scented showers from out of the thin air.

"No, no," Florizella said crossly. "I meant a pair of spectacles."

The royal enchanter waved his wand again. There was another small explosion and at once there was a huge Ferris wheel with dancing girls waving and singing from the swinging chairs, a showboat paddling its way up the chalky road with people tap-dancing on the top deck, and a flying circus high in the sky with beautiful girls and handsome men standing on the wings of little biplanes which trailed coloured smoke and flags. There was a brass band, a troupe of clowns, a magician pulling out of every pocket coloured doves, which flew around in circling flocks, and about a hundred milk-white horses cantering round a circus ring.

"No! No!" Florizella said. "A pair of spectacles to help someone who is short-sighted."

"Oh, sorry," the royal enchanter said. With a puff of blue smoke the whole thing disappeared as suddenly as it had come.

"I say, Florizella, that looked rather fun," the king said wistfully.

"I need spectacles for the giant," Florizella said. "He is most dreadfully short-sighted, and until he can see properly he cannot go back to his own land and plant his own garden."

"I can't do that sort. It's a bit scientific for me," the royal enchanter said.

"Is it possible to make spectacles big enough to fit a giant?" Florizella asked.

"I don't see why not," the royal surveyor offered. "It's just a question of making ordinary spectacles only ten times bigger."

"Can we do it?" Bennett asked.

The royal surveyor took a gold pencil from behind his ear and a piece of paper from his pocket and started doing sums for a long time, whistling softly to himself while he worked.

"If everyone in the Seven Kingdoms donated a window from every household we would have enough glass," he said after a long while.

He held up his hand for silence and did his sums again. "If everyone donated a bit of their garden gates we would have enough metal for the frames," he said.

He did some more sums. "If we emptied one of the small pools at the edge of the Great Valley lake, and then filled it with all the window panes, and then made an enormous bonfire with all the wood from Bear Forest on top and set fire to it, keeping it stoked up all the time, we could melt the glass and the melted glass would form into

133

the right sort of shape for lenses for spectacles."

The king and queen gaped. "Burn the wood from Bear Forest?" they asked. "Empty the pools at the edge of Great Valley lake?"

"Great Valley Lake is empty already," Bennett said apologetically. "We made it into lemonade and he drank it. Sorry."

"This *is* an emergency," Florizella said. "If he can't see to plant his seeds he can't look after himself. If he can't find his way home we'll never get rid of him. And everyone called him stupid at school which isn't fair. And he *is* awfully nice."

"Oh, very well," the king said. "Send out a royal proclamation. But people aren't going to like it."

In fact, people did not mind so very much. It is a rule in the Seven Kingdoms that anything you do not need is collected and shared. Empty bottles are washed and reused. Cardboard and paper is collected and mashed up and made into new paper. Even potato peelings and bits of vegetables and food are collected and fed to the herds of pigs, cows, and horses. If someone has a bicycle they don't use, they just paint it yellow and leave it outside their door. When someone else wants a ride they take it, and then leave it outside *their* door. Once people got the idea that there were plenty of bicycles around, they forgot all about stealing them and keeping them for their own. So the suggestion that since the whole kingdom had a problem with the giant, the whole kingdom had to do something about it, was not a great shock. Everyone saw at once that one window each was a small price to pay to get rid of the giant. And anyway, the summer was very fine with no rain, so they did not miss their windows as much as they would have done if it had been winter.

Everyone who had fancy iron gates cut the knobs and twiddly bits off the top and brought them to a great heap of scrap iron beside the royal camp on the Plain Green Plains. They were sorry for the short-sighted giant; but more than anything else they all hoped that the plan to make him spectacles would work, so that he could go home and grow his own crops, instead of eating so much of the food belonging to the Land of the Seven Kingdoms.

If the Seven Kingdoms had been an ordinary kind of place there would have been loads of broken bottles and scrap iron anyway. But for years they had only made exactly what they needed, and no more. "Which is all very well under ordinary circumstances," the king said crossly. "But when you have a giant arriving for an indefinite stay you like to have a bit of surplus."

The royal surveyor had surveyed the dry bottom of the pool at the edge of the Great Valley Lake.

"It's perfect," he said. "The glass in spectacles helps people to see because it is made slightly curved. The picture of the outside world is bent by the glass before the eye even sees it. The bottom of the lake is exactly the right curve. When the glass is melted by the fire and then cools and sets hard it will be exactly the right curve for the giant's eyesight."

All the members of the court and the royal guard and the people of the Plain Green Plains piled half the window panes into the lake, and half the wood on top. Then they lit the wood and let it burn and burn for two whole days and nights. All the children from Great Valley Lake School took another couple of days off without asking and had a barbecue round the lakeside which went on for two and a half days.

They had never had a summer like it.

After two days and two nights the fires burned down and the glass, which had melted under the heat, started to set solid again in the shape of the pool – flat on top and perfectly smoothly curved on the bottom. When the royal surveyor brushed the grey wood ash away, all the glass had melted into a smooth surface like ice on a pond.

Very carefully, without breaking it, they levered the glass from the bed of the pool and laid it on the soft grass of the Plain Green Plains. Then they put in the rest of the window panes and melted them too. All the children from Great Valley School took another couple of days off without permission. When they had finished they had two giant lenses for spectacles so big and so thick that it took four men to carry each one.

All that was left to do *then*, was for all the nearby blacksmiths to come with their forges, and heat and hammer all the twiddly bits from the fancy garden gates into a smart but simple pair of frames for the spectacles. Six blacksmiths rolled up in their blackened and dirty wagons and put all their forges together to make one really big hot fire. And all the blacksmiths' sons – who also should have been in school – puffed on the bellows and made the charcoal of the forges glow a bright and brilliant red. Then the blacksmiths took all the old scrap metal and hammered and bashed it, cooled it down and heated it up, twisted it and forged it, knotted it together and smoothed it out until . . .

"Done at last," said Princess Florizella with enormous relief.

It had been nearly a week since they had first met the giant and all that time

Florizella had been riding Jellybean up to the lake, and back to the royal camp, off round the countryside to find more blacksmiths, to find more metal, and out every day to find more food for the giant.

That was the bit that Samson liked the best. He always sat beside the giant at mealtimes and he had never eaten so well in his life. Crumbs of bread and cake the size of boulders fell round him. Scraps of meat pies or cheese as big as cartwheels came tumbling down. Samson the wolf cub was the only one

in the whole kingdom who was enjoying the giant's stay. He thought Giant Simon was just wonderful.

Once a day Bennett sounded a horn and the whole area for a kilometre round the giant was cleared of every person and every animal so that he could stand up and stretch. Only Cecilia stayed with him while he moved about. He had a little pocket in his shirt and he tucked Cecilia inside, to keep her safe.

"Aren't you at all nervous with him?" Bennett asked her. She was, after all, such a very little girl.

"Thilly," she said scornfully. "He ith an abtholute thweety-pie."

Bennett had to cough and go behind a tree again. But Florizella's mind was on the spectacles, which were rumbling towards them on a specially built wagon drawn by six big plough-horses. Trailing a plume of chalky white dust behind it, the wagon came down the road towards the giant.

"I think I can see it!" the giant called. "I think I can see the wagon coming! I see a white blob coming along the road!"

"Hold still! Hold still!" Florizella shrieked as the giant boots stamped the ground in excitement. "Stand still, Giant Simon!"

The giant obediently froze – but if you looked upwards you could see his thick green-socked knees trembling with excitement.

"I think I can see my spectacles!" he said as quietly as he could manage. "On a big cart. Are they really going to make me see everything clearly?"

"Yes!" Florizella said, with her fingers crossed behind her back for luck.

"And then you can go home and plant your own food," Bennett reminded him.

"And no one will ever call you stupid again," Florizella said encouragingly.

The wagon drew to a standstill at the giant's feet. Simon bent down very carefully. He put Cecilia on the ground beside Florizella and Bennett and then he picked up the spectacles by the frames and looked at them.

"Put them carefully on your nose," Florizella urged.

There was a long exciting silence while the giant settled them on his nose, pushed the arms of the spectacles into his curly fair hair, and tucked them behind his huge ears.

He gazed out across the Plain Green Plains. "I can see!" he said softly. "I can see properly at last. It's lovely. I can see the hills and the mountains behind them. I can see the trees."

He turned his big face to look downwards. "And I can see my friends . . ." he started softly . . .

Then he screamed in absolute terror – so loudly that Florizella, Bennett, Cecilia and all the royal court were blown over and over by the blast . . .

"Humans! Humans! Ugh! Humans! I hate humans! I thought you were mice!"

"Stand still! Stand still!" Florizella and Bennett yelled, as the giant tried clumsily to jump away from the royal camp while the king and queen and the royal surveyor and the whole court clung to bushes and trees as the whole world shook round them. "You'll hurt us! Stand still!"

The plough-horses threw up their heads and bolted in six different directions at once. Their driver leaped clear of the wagon, which overturned and was dragged zigzagging wildly away. People ran screaming with terror as the mighty boots crashed down first in one spot and then in another, like great unpredictable thunderbolts. High, high above them, above the tops of the trees, they could hear the roaring complaints of the frightened giant.

"I hate humans! I hate humans! They're 'orrible! 'Orrible! I hate them. They're dangerous! They're nasty! They're sneaky! They come after you when you ain't done nothing! 'Orrible! 'Orrible!"

"Stand still!" Florizella yelled. "Stand still and listen for a moment!"

The giant forced himself to stand still, quivering all over with fright.

"We're not 'orrible," Florizella said. "I mean horrible. We've been kind to you – remember? We've made you these spectacles and it took all the glass we had and all the iron! We've fed you every day! We're not sneaky and nasty!"

The giant shook his head. He was hopelessly confused.

"Cecilia is a human," Florizella gabbled at the top of her voice. "And you like her. She tells you wonderful stories. And you like Bennett – he brought you lemonade when you were thirsty. And you like me – and all of us here. We've fed you for a week. We've cared for you."

The giant shook his head.

"I don't believe you! I've heard all about you! It was one of your tricks – being nice to me. I know all about humans! You'd have tied me up when I was asleep or something sneaky like that! You'd have come climbing up beanstalks after me! You'd steal my gold or set other giants on me! Well, you watch out, Princess Florizella! Fee-fi-fo-fum, you know! I am a giant after all! I can grind your bones, don't forget!

Fee-fi-fo-fum!
Fee-fi-fo-fum!

I can't remember how the rest of it goes ... Umpty-umpty-umpty-um!"

He finished the last "umpty-umpty-umpty-um!" with a great roar, trying very hard to hide his own fear and to frighten everyone else.

"What are you going to do?" Florizella demanded of Bennett in an urgent whisper. "If he goes on about grinding bones the royal guard won't like it at all! And then we'll have a little war on our hands."

"A giant war you mean," Bennett said. "And *we've* given him spectacles so he can see us. We won't have a chance if he attacks!"

Florizella looked behind her. Already people were getting up and looking for weapons, and grouping round the king and queen. They all looked angry and frightened. The royal guard gathered to the royal standard with their hands on their swords. The drummer girls were looking for their drumsticks in a hurry in case anyone wanted to sound the retreat – or even advance. The queen beckoned urgently to Florizella to come to her. Florizella smiled pleasantly and waved back, pretending not to understand.

Suddenly Cecilia, the very little girl, pushed between Florizella and Bennett.

"Lift me up!" she demanded. "Lift me up on your shoulder."

Bennett picked her up. She was still only as high as the giant's laces on his monstrous boots.

"Thimon!" she yelled. "Giant Thimon! Can you hear me?"

The giant stopped still at her commanding little squeak. "Yes," he said a little more softly. "I can hear you, Thethilia."

"You are a big thilly to thpeak to Florithella like that," she said severely. "She hath been ath nithe ath she could be. And then you thtart up thith fee-fi-fo-fum nonthenth. You should be ashamed of yourthelf. You are a great big naughty thing."

"I . . ." the giant began, but it was no use. Cecilia was quite unstoppable.

"Now, you thay thorry," she said firmly. "Or no one ith going to talk to you."

There was a long silence. "THAY THORRY!" Cecilia shouted with infinite threat.

"Thorry," the giant said. "I mean, sorry. I was startled. I've never talked with humans before. I thought you were all horrid little vermin that climb up beansprouts to steal money and murder innocent giants. A race of burglars and killers. I thought you were all called Jack."

"That's just a fairy story," Florizella said.

"Sorry," the giant said more softly. "I thought it was true. I thought we were natural enemies."

Bennett shook his head. "There are no natural enemies," he said. "You can always be friends if you choose to be. We'd like to be friends with you."

The giant shuffled his feet, rather dangerously.

"I'm sorry," he said again very humbly. "I want to be friends. I was very frightened for a moment, that was all."

"That'th better," Cecilia said firmly.

The giant bent down and put out his big warm hand. The three children climbed into it. He lifted them up and up and up, past the tree trunks, past the high branches of the trees, past the birds' nests and the tops of the trees. Up to his face.

His big blue eyes were huge behind his new specs, as big as two blue harvest moons. The effect was quite startling: Florizella found she was gazing and gazing into his deep, enormous eyes.

"I *am* sorry," he said again. "I know you're nice now. But I was always taught humans were dreadful."

"There are good and bad," Cecilia said. "Jutht like giantth, jutht like all people."

Florizella and Bennett exchanged an amazed look.

"This Cecilia is one smart little girl," Bennett whispered to Florizella. Aloud he said, "If you are ready to leave, Giant Simon, then we have some vegetables and seeds and plants for you." He pointed towards the horizon where there was a long train of carts loaded high with sacks of tomato seeds, lettuce seeds, carrot seeds, potato seeds, marrow seeds, cucumber seeds, corn on the cob seeds, parsnip seeds, and behind them more wagons piled high with little fruit trees, their branches tossing with the rolling of the carts along the road.

The giant gave a little sigh of pleasure. The three children grabbed on to his thumb and no one was blown away.

"That's a wonderful sight," he said. "It's very kind of you. I shall take them and plant them and my garden will be the best of all gardens. And then I shall have friends who will come round to see it. They won't call me stupid then! They'll be pleased to know me!"

He bent down and put the children softly on the ground. With delicate fingers he picked up the tiny vegetables out of the carts and looked at them carefully. He could see them properly at last. "These are grand!" he said. "Grand. I'm very grateful to you all."

"It's our pleasure," the king said graciously. "And now I think it is probably time for you to go, Giant Simon."

It was a little unfortunate that everyone nodded very enthusiastically at the prospect of the giant leaving.

"We will be sorry to lose you," the queen said tactfully. "But I expect you will want to be getting back to your garden. Autumn is coming, you will want to be getting the ground ready for your crops."

"We'll point you in the direction of your home," Bennett said. "You came from the west, from over the mountains."

The giant had gone very quiet.

"We'll send the wagons along behind you," Florizella said cheerfully. "They can follow you until they reach our borders, and then you can carry the seeds and trees to your home."

The giant said nothing. He sighed deeply. All the flags at the royal camp streamed out in the wind of his sigh. A few tents blew over.

"Watch out," Bennett said to Florizella. "I think he's getting tearful."

A fat solitary tear crashed down into the bushes beside the two children, like a single massive wave on a beach.

"Don't cry!" Florizella yelled desperately. "What's the matter?"

"Hold the horses!" Bennett shouted to the royal camp. "Fasten down the tents! Prepare for a storm!"

"Unh-hunh!"

The ground rocked with the giant's sob.

"Unh-hunh! Unh-hunh!"

"What *is* it?" Florizella shouted upwards.

"I'm going to miss you!"

The giant was bawling like a baby.

"I'm going to have to go back to my own country all by

myself, and no one will tell me stories there."

Tears cascaded down upon the children and the royal camp like a hurricane, like a typhoon. The giant's sobs uprooted great trees, a tent was washed away, several flagpoles were snapped off, the banners swept away on the gale of his cries.

High above the noise a little voice was raised. "Thtop it!" said Cecilia indignantly. "A great big giant like you! You should be ashamed of yourthelf!"

Abruptly the giant stopped crying.

"You are too big to be thquealing and thnivelling all the time," Cecilia said firmly. "Bethideth, there ith no need for it. I am coming back with you to your country. I have athked my mum and she thayth I can. We can plant your garden together. I will thtay with you till the end of the thummer holidayth. And Florithella and Bennett will vithit you when you are thettled again."

"Will you?" the giant asked. "Will you come with me, Thethilia? Stay with me until the end of the summer? And will you visit me, Florizella and Bennett?"

The children shouted, "Yes, of course! Of course we will!" and watched anxiously as the giant wiped the last tears from his eyes with the back of his hand.

"I tell you what! We'll have a party to see you off!" the king shouted up. "I expect you'd like some fireworks, wouldn't you? A nice jolly farewell party?"

"With hats?" Giant Simon asked eagerly. "And things that you blow that squeal? And streamers? And games?"

Florizella and Bennett looked reproachfully at the king. "Oh, Daddy, look what you've done," Florizella said reproachfully. "How on *earth* are you going to make him a party hat? Or a blower?"

"Sorry," the king said. "I was just thinking of the royal enchanter's spectacular show."

"Oh, yes!" Florizella said delightedly. "It's not like any party you've ever seen before!" she yelled up at the giant. "No hats, but the most wonderful things! You must wait till you see it!"

153

The royal enchanter stepped forward. His magic blue coat billowed round him, his tall pointy hat was slightly askew. "An amusing little something?" he asked the king with a smile.

"Something for the children," the king said. "They've been so good!"

The royal enchanter produced a long silvery wand from his drooping sleeve and tapped it lightly on the ground. At once a white marble fountain sprang out of the ground, bubbling and flowing with raspberry soda. Fireworks leaped out of the grass and whizzed up into the evening sky, popping and twinkling in a million different colours. The showboat which had so caught the king's fancy earlier, came pounding up the road with its paddles turning and very loud music and dancing on the top deck. A dozen incredibly fast, incredibly slippery water-slides appeared from nowhere and the children from the Great Valley School (*never* had they had such a summer!) dashed for them and flung themselves, still fully dressed, up the steps and then screaming, round and round, head over heels, down the waterslides. A little steam engine with carriages came chuffing up the road and high-kicking dancing girls wrapped in feather boas sprang out of every door and danced up and down. A thousand parachutes opened in the sky above them and a regimental brass band floated lightly down playing ragtime jazz, never missing a note, even when they dropped to the ground and rolled. High on the crest of the billowing blue wave, a dozen world-class surfers came dipping and wheeling, riding the high plumes of sea spray through the little forest.

"Now *that's* what I call a spectacle!" the royal enchanter said to the royal surveyor with a superior sort of smile.

But Florizella had something on her mind. She looked round the crowd of laughing delighted faces until she saw Cecilia's mother. She was laughing and pointing at a circus which had just arrived. There were unicorns doing a water ballet in rainbow-coloured water, with flying horses dipping and wheeling round rose-pink fountains.

"I say," Florizella asked. "Is it really all right for Cecilia to go with the giant?"

"Oh, yes," she said with a smile. "She's always been a great one for pets, has Cecilia. She'll stay till he's settled in and then she'll come home again. I let her go away for the holidays as long as she is back in time for school."

"Pets?" Florizella asked. "Does Cecilia call Giant Simon a pet?"

"Oh, yes," the woman said. "Now all my children want one."

Florizella shook her head. "I just hope it doesn't become a craze," she said. "I don't think we can manage more than one a year!"

"Let them go, Florizella," Bennett said. "If she has decided that Giant Simon is her pet then she'll insist on keeping him. I'd rather she went with him than decided that she should keep him here. That is one little girl who gets her own way!" He cupped his hands round his mouth and shouted upwards. "Well, goodbye, Giant Simon. We'll come and see you in the autumn."

"Goodbye!"

the giant boomed down at them. Fireworks exploded behind his head and he laughed delightedly.

"Goodbye everyone, and thank you for everything, especially the party!"

"Tho long!" Cecilia called from high up in the giant's pocket. "I'll be home in time for thchool in the autumn!"

The huge giant and the little girl in his pocket waved to the royal court and to Princess Florizella and Prince Bennett and then, with the wagons of seeds and trees following behind him, the giant turned westward into the pale apricot evening sunlight and carefully stepped his way home.

The Mum-Minder

Jacqueline Wilson

Sadie's mum is a child-minder. As well as looking after Sadie and her baby sister, Sara, she also takes care of Gemma, Vincent and baby Clive while their mums work. But what happens when it is the child-minder who needs to be looked after? Sadie is about to find out!

You'll never guess what! I've been a *real* policewoman today. Gemma's mum took me to work with her. And her Gemma. And our Sara. And Vincent and little Clive. All of us.

My mum has got flu. Gemma's mum drove her to the doctor's last night. Mum's got to stay in bed today and tomorrow and the next day. So has Nan. She's got it too.

"I can't have flu. I'm never ill," Mum moaned. "I can't let you all down. I've got to look after the kids."

"Well, you *are* ill, whether we like it or not," said Gemma's mum. "And you've never let us down before. You've always looked after our kids. So we've got to stick together, like Sadie said."

"That's right. And it's OK. *I'll* look after the babies," I said. I was feeling bad about leaving Mum to cope on her own and I was desperate to make up for it.

"It's sweet of you to offer, Sadie, but you're only a kid yourself, love," said Gemma's mum.

I got a bit annoyed at that. I'm not a kid, I'm nearly nine for goodness sake, and Mum says I'm old for my age. I look after Sara enough times. If you can cope with our Sara then other babies are a doddle. Gemma's quite a sensible little kid at times, and Vincent's OK if you keep an eye on him – well, two eyes plus one in the back of your head – and baby Clive doesn't yell *all* the time.

But Gemma's mum and Vincent's mum and

Clive's mum and even *my* mum wouldn't listen to me. They said I couldn't cope.

"We're the ones who are going to have to cope," said Gemma's mum.

"But how?" said Vincent's mum. "I can't leave Vincent with a neighbour because they go out to work too."

"My mother-in-law always said she'd look after any babies if I had to go back to work, but the first time she looked after Clive he cried all the time and she said Never Again," said Clive's mum. "She couldn't manage."

"We're going to have to manage," said Gemma's mum. "It's only for this week. Can't anyone take three days off work? I would, but I've used up all my leave."

Vincent's mum and Clive's mum couldn't take time off either.

"Then just this once we'll have to take the kids to work with us," said Gemma's mum.

"How on earth could I have the babies in my office?" said Vincent's mum.

"You can't have kids cooped up behind the chocolate counter all day," said Clive's mum.

"I'll look after them as usual," my mum

croaked. "I can go to bed when they have their naps and—"

"Nonsense," said Gemma's mum. "Now listen. Tomorrow *I'll* have the kids. They can come to the police station with me. Then Thursday they can go uptown to your office and Friday go to the shop. I know it's going to be difficult but we'll just have to give it a whirl."

I still feel like I'm whirling. And it's great great great!

I got up ever so early and gave Sara a baby bottle to keep her quiet while I got washed and dressed, and then I made Mum a cup of tea and some toast for her breakfast. Then I heated up some tomato soup at the same time and poured in into a vacuum flask.

"That's your lunch, Mum," I explained, when I'd woken her and propped a couple of pillows behind her. "And look, I've brought some apples and biscuits up, and the kettle and the coffee and Sara's Ribena because I think you need the vitamin C more than she does."

"You're a real pal, Sadie," Mum mumbled.

"So where are you going today then? Round to Rachel's?"

"You must be joking! I'll have to go to the police station with Gemma's mum. She'll never cope with the babies on her own."

You can say that again.

She looked a bit fussed when she came to pick us up.

"Me and my big mouth," she said. "I haven't a clue what my boss is going to say. I don't *think* there's anything in Police Orders about not bringing your children and all their little friends to work with you, but I kind of get the feeling it's going to be frowned on."

Gemma's mum's Police Inspector boss did frown when he saw all of us. His eyebrows practically knitted together.

"What on earth are you playing at, WPC Parsons?" he said.

"Oh, sir," said Gemma's mum, and she started gabbling this long, involved, apologetic explanation, while Gemma scuffed her shoes and Vincent picked his nose and Sara struggled in my arms and Clive cried in his carrycot.

162

"This is ridiculous," said the Inspector. "You're a policewoman, not Mary Blooming Poppins. I can't have my police station turned into a nursery, not even for one day. You must take them all home with you right this minute."

Sara had stopped struggling. She was staring up at the Inspector. Then she gave him a big sunny smile.

"Dad-Dad!" she announced delightedly.

The Inspector looked shocked.

"I'm not your Dad-Dad," he said.

"*Dad-Dad!*" Sara insisted, and held out her chubby arms to him.

It's not her fault. We don't often see our dad. Sara's only little and she makes mistakes.

The Inspector was big and he looked as if he'd never made a mistake in his life – but he made one right that minute. His arms reached out of their own accord. Sara snuggled up to him happily.

"Dad-Dad," she announced smugly, patting his cheek.

He still tried to frown, but he couldn't stop his mouth going all smiley.

"Is this your little girl, WPC Parsons?" he asked.

"No, sir. This one's mine. Gemma. Say hello to the Inspector, Gemma," said Gemma's mum.

Gemma wasn't going to let Sara get all the attention. She smiled determinedly at the Inspector, tossing her curls.

"Hello, Mr Inspector Man. I've come to work with Mummy."

"Well. Just for today," said the Inspector, picking her up too.

Gemma's mum winked at me. It looked like it was going to be OK after all.

"How would you like a ride in my police car, eh?" said the Inspector.

"Me too, me too, me too!" said Vincent, tugging at the Inspector's trouser leg.

Clive let out a long, loud wail from his carrycot.

"He's practising being a police siren," I said.

The Inspector looked at me.

"You're not one of the babies," he said.

"I should think not," I said indignantly.

"I'm here to keep them all in order."

"I'm glad to hear it. It looks as if it's going to be some undertaking," said the Inspector. "We'd better give you a bit of authority."

He found me a policewoman's hat and a special tie and a big badge.

"There we go. Now you're head of my Child Protection Team. What's your name?"

"Sadie, Sir," I added, and I gave him a little salute.

"I'm glad you've reported for duty, WPC Sadie," he said. "Right, I'll give you your orders. Quieten the baby. Wipe the little boy's nose – my trousers are getting rather damp. And take these two little treasures from me so that I can give you a proper salute back."

Gemma jumped down happily enough but Sara screamed when I tried to take her.

"Dad-Dad!" she insisted furiously – and that poor nice-after-all Inspector had to carry her around all day long.

We had a wonderful time. The Inspector really did take us out in a big police car. He wouldn't go very fast but he did put the siren on just for a second. That was another mistake. Vincent made very loud police-siren noises all day after that, and Clive did his best to accompany him.

We had Coke and crisps back in the police canteen and then, when Gemma's mum had to do some work, the Inspector took us to see a great big police dog. Gemma didn't like him and Vincent was a bit worried, but Sara laughed and patted him.

"Yes, nice doggy," said the Inspector.

"Nice Dad-Dad," said Sara.

She's dead artful, my little baby sister. Like

I said, she insisted on staying with the Inspector, even when he had to parade some policemen and inspect some prisoners in the cells. Sara smiled all the time and the policemen and even the prisoners smiled back.

Gemma and Vincent were both getting a bit restless – and baby Clive was very restless indeed. I was tempted to leave him in one of the prisoners' cells, but one of the canteen ladies plucked him up in her arms and started cooing at him. She gave him a little lick of her special syrup pudding and it sweetened him up considerably.

I left Clive with the canteen lady and played prisoners with Gemma and Vincent, and a friendly policeman showed me how to take their fingerprints with wonderful gungy black ink. Vincent particularly enjoyed the procedure. He didn't just put his fingerprints on the pad. He put them on his knees and his nose and the desk and even up the wall.

The friendly policeman had to carry him off to be scrubbed. I paraded Gemma up and down the corridors and into the control-room and another friendly policeman showed us how to work his computer so that lots of squiggly green information flashed up on the screen. Gemma thought it was better than television and sat on his lap and had a go at pressing all the buttons herself.

I left Gemma with that friendly policeman and went to see what my fellow policewoman was up to. Gemma's mum was in the front office seeing to members of the public. She let me stand up on a box and see to them too. We took particulars of a stolen purse and Gemma's mum showed me how to fill in a crime sheet. She said I did it very neatly. I think it's all the practice writing in this diary. I've been writing and writing and writing today since we got back home.

Mum's in bed. Sara's in bed too. She was still saying Dad-Dad as she drifted off to sleep. That Inspector says he's not her Dad-Dad but perhaps he could be a sort of uncle and come and visit her some time. He's not a bit frowny and fierce when you get to know him. I think I'll maybe go and work full-time for him when I'm grown up.

The Magic Parrot

Judy Corbalis

Aunt Hilda was at home when Sam came in after school. He'd been hoping she'd be out, but she was standing in the hallway with her beady black eyes snapping.

"Wipe your feet well," she said crossly. "Just look at the mud on your trousers."

Sam kept his hands behind his back.

"What have you got behind your back, Sam?" asked Aunt Hilda.

"Nothing," said Sam quickly. "Just a box, that's all."

"Nonsense!" Aunt Hilda was scornful. "Nobody goes round collecting empty boxes. What's in it?"

"Nothing," repeated Sam desperately.

"Well, put it on the hall table then," she said, "and go in and get your tea quietly and quickly. I have a dreadful headache."

Aunt Hilda was always suffering from bad headaches. Sam had to be quiet in the house and tiptoe around and remember not to slam doors, and he could never ever have other children in to play because their noise might disturb Aunt Hilda and make her headaches worse.

He put his box down very carefully on the table and, crossing his fingers, he began to open the kitchen door.

Aunt Hilda looked at the box. Sam looked at Aunt Hilda. Very slowly the lid rose and a tiny brown face with little pointed ears and long long whiskers peeped out.

Aunt Hilda screamed and screamed. She rushed upstairs crying and shouting.

"Take it away! Get rid of it *at once*, you horrid, wicked boy."

Poor Sam seized the little hamster and, tucking it into his coat pocket, went into the kitchen and sadly ate his tea. The hamster climbed out of his pocket and sat on the table. Sam gave it some breadcrumbs and stroked its head. The hamster sat up and looked at him. Its fur was all soft and fluffy.

"She'll never let me keep it now," thought Sam. Then he wondered whether, if he promised to keep it in his room and never let it downstairs, Aunt Hilda and Uncle George might, just this once, let him have it after all.

He sat stroking the hamster for a long time until finally he heard Uncle George's key in the front door. He could hear voices on the stairs. Aunt Hilda's loud and angry, Uncle George's lower and soothing. Uncle George's footsteps came towards the kitchen. Sam put the hamster back in his pocket and put his hand over it to keep it safe.

The door opened.

Uncle George stood there looking very annoyed.

"Sam," he thundered, "I am extremely angry with you. You've upset your aunt and told her a lie. And you've brought a rodent into this house."

"It *isn't* a rodent," said Sam tearfully. "It's

a baby hamster. This boy at school gave it to me. I'll look after it myself and it doesn't eat much and I'll pay for it out of my pocket money. *Please, please*, Uncle George."

"Certainly not. What an idea!" snorted Uncle George. "Hamsters *are* rodents: they're dirty and unpleasant and you're not keeping one here. Take it straight back to that boy! And as soon as you're home, go upstairs and apologize to your aunt."

And he went out.

Sam sat at the table looking at his hamster with tears in his eyes. He did want a pet so much. He wasn't allowed a dog or a cat, Uncle George had said a rabbit or a guinea pig would smell, and this hamster had seemed so perfect.

The hamster began to wash its face with its paws.

"I wish I could keep you," said Sam sadly. And he tucked it back in his pocket and slowly set off with it.

When he got home again, he went straight out to the far end of the back garden and climbed up the old apple tree. As he sat there feeling sad and lonely, he heard footsteps. Looking up at him was Blackbeard Smith, his aunt and uncle's gardener.

Blackbeard Smith lived in the big shed at the bottom of the garden. He kept the garden tidy and cleaned the car and did odd jobs round the house. Aunt Hilda didn't like him at all.

"It's ridiculous having a gardener like that. Of course he can't work properly," she used to say.

For the really interesting thing about Blackbeard Smith, apart from his wooden leg and the hook he had instead of a hand, was that he was a real live retired pirate. Sam had seen it on one of his letters once.

"B.B. Smith
Pirate (Retd.)"

Aunt Hilda had wanted to get rid of Blackbeard, but he came with the house.

"You can't do it, I'm afraid, my dear," Uncle George had said firmly.

Sam was strictly forbidden to go near Blackbeard's shed or to "bother" him at all but, in fact, he quite often talked to Blackbeard while the pirate was working in the garden, and he had a secret ambition to see inside his shed. Blackbeard was tall with a bushy beard and a glittering eye. Sam felt it would have been terrifying to have met him in his pirate clothes.

"Did you have a sword between your teeth?" he had asked Blackbeard once.

"Did I? Did I ever, young lad," roared Blackbeard. "A sword in me teeth and another in me hand and a revolver in me belt."

Sam had shuddered with fright at the thought.

Another mysterious thing about Blackbeard Smith was where he went for his holidays. Every year, he would pack up a case and leave for a holiday. He always came back, but he would never say where he'd been. Aunt Hilda got very cross.

"How ridiculous," she said. "Of course we should know where he's going. What if there's an emergency?"

But there never was and Blackbeard Smith would never tell.

"I'm staying with an old friend," was all he would say.

Sam looked at the pirate through the branches.

Blackbeard Smith winked up at him.

"It's a beautiful evening," he called cheerily.

Sam glowered down. "No, it's not."

Blackbeard Smith ran his hook menacingly across the tree trunk.

"Sulking, are we?" he enquired. "Moody, are we? What's on our mind, then? Come down and tell the scourge of the South Sea Clippers what the matter is."

Sam crawled unhappily down the tree trunk.

"I'm in the wrong family," he muttered gloomily. "I hate them."

"One way or another," said Blackbeard Smith, "we're all in the wrong family. So what's the problem with them now?"

"They won't let me keep my hamster," blurted out Sam, and he began to cry. "I haven't got *any* pets. Not a white mouse, not a kitten, not nothing."

"Not *anything*," corrected Blackbeard. "You may not have a pet, you may be disappointed in life, but for goodness' sake speak proper, boy."

Sam sniffed.

"You'd better come in and sit down and we'll see what we can come up with," said Blackbeard, and he led Sam into his big shed.

This was the moment Sam had been waiting for for months.

They stepped inside and Sam saw that the shed was divided into three rooms. Blackbeard pushed open a door and Sam was inside the first retired pirate's sitting room he'd ever seen in his life.

"I don't believe it," he breathed.

"Look around, look around," said Blackbeard expansively. "I'll just go off and slip into something more comfortable."

And while Sam tried the telescope and inspected the room generally, the old pirate stumped off to his back room.

Five minutes later he was back.

"Incredible!" cried Sam.

"And this," announced Blackbeard Smith grandly, pulling a photograph from behind the armadillo shell, "is my former parrot, Cocky Smart, Retired."

"Retired where?" Sam was curious.

"Where?" cried Blackbeard Smith. "This boy asked me where! Now where would you think a parrot would retire to? Eastbourne? Too northerly! Blackpool? Too political! Weymouth? Too many day trippers! Chipping Sodbury? Too rural! The Zoo? Of course not! Use your intelligence, boy. Where would a parrot retire to?"

"I don't know," said poor Sam.

"The West Indies, of course. Where else? Set himself up nicely in a banana tree near Kingston. Got himself a pretty wife and a fine clutch of eggs, which hatched into a colourful family of six."

"And that's where you go every year!"

"Of course, boy," boomed Blackbeard Smith. "Every summer, it's off to the West Indies to spend a month with Cocky Smart. Now there's not too many retired pirates can boast they're invited by their former parrots to spend the summer holidays, I can tell you."

Sam was impressed.

"He looks very nice," he said, looking at the parrot's photograph. "Look at the way he's looking at you. That's the kind of pet *I'd* like."

Blackbeard Smith struck a match against his wooden leg and lit his pipe thoughtfully.

"And why shouldn't you?" he asked after a while. "And why not, then? Mind, it would have to be specially worked out. Go home now, boy, and apologize to your aunt, and come down here and see me this time tomorrow."

Sam could hardly wait. He arrived promptly at Blackbeard's shed next day and knocked on the door. Blackbeard took him into the marvellous sitting room and handed him a glass.

"Have a quick shot of this, boy," he said. "Afternoon tea."

And he winked at Sam.

Sam swallowed a large mouthful. A terrible burning seized his throat. He coughed and spat and spluttered.

"What is it?"

"Rum, boy, rum," said the old pirate. "Builds growing boys. Now if you just sit tight here I've got something next door you're going to be very pleased to see."

Sam sat down gratefully. He was feeling rather dizzy from the effects of the rum.

"Close your eyes," shouted Blackbeard from outside the door.

Sam's eyes were already shut. The rum had made them sting.

"Open them now!"

Sam decided he was feeling better. He opened his eyes cautiously and saw, sitting on the pirate's shoulder, a strange object covered by a tea towel.

"Pull it off, boy," growled Blackbeard Smith. Sam lifted off the tea towel.

Underneath sat a beautiful shiny metal parrot.

"Oh!" cried Sam. "*It's wonderful.*"

"He's yours," said Blackbeard Smith.

And he lifted the parrot on to Sam's shoulder.

"Made him meself last night. Have a good close look at him now."

Sam was overjoyed.

"He's fantastic. I love him. Oh thank you, Blackbeard, thank you."

"Just take good care of him, that's all," muttered the old pirate. "Now off you go. I've got summer holiday packing to do. Can't find me spare hook anywhere."

Sam went racing out to the street, his parrot on his shoulder.

"Look, everybody, look!" he shouted. "*I've* got a pet. A fantastic parrot."

Sam's parrot was a great success. He took him to school next morning.

"His name's Achilles," he told his friends at morning playtime and they all took turns at stroking the parrot.

"Where did you get him?" asked David.

"It's a secret," said Sam. "But I can tell you a man I know gave him to me."

Achilles' fame spread.

After school everyone wanted to walk home with Sam and carry Achilles for him.

Sam kept Achilles firmly on his own shoulder.

"He's new to me," he explained. "He has to get used to me. I can't go handing him round to everyone, or he'll get frightened."

"Can I come to tea?" asked David when they got to Sam's gate.

Sam hesitated. He was longing to have David in and to show off Achilles and let him meet Blackbeard Smith. But he remembered Aunt Hilda's cross look and thought better of it.

"I'm not allowed to have people to tea," he said. "It's my aunt. She gets headaches easily."

David was disappointed.

"Well, bring Achilles out later," he said. "And let me have *one* turn with him. I am supposed to be your best friend, after all."

"You are," Sam assured him.

He took Achilles out after tea and they took turns with him on their shoulders. When he got home, Sam saw Blackbeard in the garden. He and Achilles rushed down to the shed.

"Look, Blackbeard," cried Sam. "He's really good. Everybody likes him and he sits on *my* shoulder all the time and look how he looks at me. Just like Cocky Smart."

"And what does your aunt say, then?" queried the pirate.

"*She* thinks he's just a toy. She doesn't know he's a real pet," said Sam.

"All to the good, boy," remarked Blackbeard Smith. "And I shouldn't tell her meself if I were you. Now, I'm off early tomorrow morning and when I come back there'll be a present from Jamaica for you. Take care of that parrot while I'm gone."

"Oh, I will!" Sam assured him. "Have a good holiday, Blackbeard."

The pirate waved his hook and disappeared into his shed.

Sam took Achilles up to his room and sat with him on the wooden bed-end.

"There's your perch," he said. "You can sleep there."

He smiled at Achilles.

Achilles winked at him.

Sam's eyes opened wide. He couldn't

possibly have seen properly.

Achilles winked again.

"Achilles!" whispered Sam softly. "Wink again."

Achilles winked.

"Go to sleep," breathed Sam.

Achilles obediently put his head under his wing.

Sam climbed into bed and fell asleep.

Next day at school he told David that Achilles could wink.

"I don't believe that." David was scornful. "He's a really good parrot but he's made of metal and he can't wink."

"He can, he can," said Sam. "At playtime I'll show you."

But Achilles refused to wink or move his head and no one believed Sam at all.

That night, Sam put Achilles on the bed-end.

"Wink!" he ordered.

Achilles winked.

"Put your head under your wing," said Sam.

Achilles did.

"He only does it with him and me around," Sam said to himself. "And I suppose maybe he'll do it with Blackbeard Smith as well, when he's back from his holiday."

Things went very nicely for the next week or so. Quite a lot of children asked Sam to tea and they all loved Achilles.

But at the end of the week something dreadful happened. It started very surprisingly.

One night Sam and Achilles went to bed as usual. Sam had been asleep for quite a long time when he was suddenly awoken by strange noises. He opened his eyes and peeped cautiously out from under the covers.

Achilles was sitting up on the end of the bed.

"Hello, Sam," he said. He had a very creaky metal voice.

"*Hallo!*" replied Sam. "You can *talk*."

"I've been listening to you and learning," creaked Achilles. "All parrots should be able to talk. And I've been singing."

"So that's what the noises were," thought Sam.

"I'm not very good yet. I'm practising," explained Achilles. "But it's used up all my energy. I'm hungry, Sam."

Sam lifted Achilles on to his shoulder and crept down to the kitchen with him.

And it was while he was searching in the cupboard for some bread and cheese for Achilles that the dreadful thing happened.

Achilles gave a creaky squawk of joy, and Sam turned round just in time to see him eating the knobs off the cooker. As Sam watched in horror, he reached out and pecked off the door handle.

"Achilles!" cried Sam in a loud whisper. "Stop it *at once!* What are you doing?"

"Mmmmm," croaked Achilles dreamily. "Delicious. Yum, yum."

And he patted his stomach contentedly with his wing.

Sam looked at the cooker, seized Achilles and rushed back up to bed as fast as he could.

Next morning there was an awful commotion.

"But how could it have happened?" asked Uncle George.

"I keep telling you I don't know, but you don't hear me." Aunt Hilda was exasperated. "What I can tell you is that it *has* happened and I can't use the cooker any more."

That night, as Sam lay in bed after his Chinese takeaway supper, he heard scuffling and creaking from the end of the bed. Sitting up, he saw Achilles climb off the bed and creep across the floor and out of the door.

Sam followed him. Somehow he thought Achilles seemed bigger and fatter. The parrot waddled into the kitchen and over to the washing machine, opened his beak, and snap, snap, he swallowed all the washing machine buttons.

Sam was horrified.

"Come *here*, Achilles," he whispered.

Achilles came creaking over to him.

"You're not to eat up anything in this kitchen," explained Sam. "We need all the buttons and knobs and things. Please, Achilles."

Achilles dreamily lifted the cheese grater

off its hook with his wing and swallowed it down.

"But I was hungry," he croaked.

Sam gave a sigh, picked him up and went back to bed.

When he woke up next morning, he took Achilles on to his shoulder. The parrot was definitely heavier and taller than he had been the day before.

"Achilles," said Sam, "all this food is making you grow. You'll be too big to sit on my shoulder if you go on eating. You've got to stop."

That night, after his Indian takeaway supper, he measured Achilles. He was five centimetres taller!

"Achilles," said Sam sternly, "YOU ARE NOT TO GO DOWN TO THE KITCHEN TONIGHT AND STEAL THINGS. Do you promise?"

Achilles put his wing on his heart.

"I promise, Sam."

Sam was woken next morning by loud shouts of dismay from his uncle and aunt's room.

"All the taps in the bathroom are missing," shouted his uncle.

"*And* the cabinet doorknobs," sobbed his aunt.

"I can't have a bath!" roared Uncle George.

"This house is haunted," wept Aunt Hilda.

Sam looked at Achilles.

Achilles was even bigger.

"You promised," he reminded him sadly.

"I know," squawked Achilles, "and I was very good. I didn't go *near* the kitchen although the cabinet doorknobs there are much bigger and I was starving."

Sam put his head in his hands. He wished Blackbeard Smith would come back soon.

Achilles wiggled his metal feathers and stroked Sam's cheek with his beak.

"I love you, Sam," he creaked.

"I know," said Sam sadly.

All day in school he couldn't concentrate. He had left Achilles hidden under the bed. Achilles was getting so much bigger, Sam couldn't carry him anywhere on his shoulder any more.

What could he do?

And Blackbeard Smith was still on holiday!

"Maybe," thought Sam, "he'll have arrived home when I get back from school today."

But as soon as he turned into his own street, he saw that something bad had happened. His uncle was standing by the gate, looking thunderous, talking to a large policeman. Sam's heart sank.

"What's happened?" he asked nervously.

"I don't know what's happening," his uncle said grimly, "but I intend to find out. Now someone's taken the lawnmower."

"But it was locked in the shed," said Sam, knowing exactly who it would be.

"That's right," said his uncle. "And it's too big to get out through the window."

Sam raced into the house and upstairs. Achilles was lying under the bed.

"Come out, *at once*," he cried.

Achilles wriggled out from under. He was at least twenty centimetres taller!

"Achilles!" shouted Sam. "*You* ate that lawnmower."

Achilles hung his head. His beak trembled.

"I know," he whispered. "I was terribly hungry."

Sam was distraught.

"Oh, Achilles, what shall I *do* with you?"

"I don't know," said Achilles humbly. "I get so hungry I can't help myself. That lawnmower was delicious. I won't need to eat again for ages."

Sam looked at him.

"If you eat any more," he warned, "you won't be able to fit under my bed and you'll have to stay outside."

An oily tear trickled down Achilles' face.

"I don't want to stay outside by myself."

"Well, *stop eating!*"

Sam picked up his football.

"I'm going out and you're not coming with me," he said. "You're staying inside. You're getting too big for my shoulder."

But Achilles looked so sad that Sam felt sorry for him and decided to carry him into the garden for a bit.

He left his parrot hidden behind the garden shed and went off to play football.

He and his friends had been playing for

about an hour when they heard a lot of noise and saw an odd procession of people coming towards the park.

At the front was a very fat, very angry woman with a small boy crying loudly beside her, and behind them came three more children, two boys on bicycles, two mothers, three fathers, a tramp, a policeman, Sam's uncle, another half dozen children, four dogs and a big tom cat. And right at the back, Sam saw, with a sinking heart, a strangely familiar figure wrapped in a large old gardening coat and cap. It was Achilles! He had gone out by himself for the first time.

The procession came into the park. The very fat woman was shouting angrily and waving her fists. Sam went up to her.

"What's the matter?" he asked.

"Matter!" shouted the woman. "I'll tell you what's the matter. Somebody's stolen his tricycle! That's what's the matter. We're all looking for the thief and when we catch him, I'll make him sorry, I can tell you."

Sam seized his football and joined the procession behind Achilles.

As soon as he could he pulled Achilles to one side.

"I was just helping them look," explained the parrot.

"Achilles!" Sam was angry. "You're telling me a lie. *You* ate that tricycle."

Achilles was embarrassed.

"How did you know?"

"Look at yourself, you stupid parrot!" shouted Sam.

"I'm not a stupid parrot," sobbed Achilles. "You said I was a fantastic parrot. And I know I'm a very hungry parrot."

"Well, you're not a fantastic parrot now. You're an enormous parrot with wheels coming out of your shoulders," cried Sam in despair. "I don't know what to feed you with, and I can't keep people from knowing it's you doing all these things for much longer."

"You don't love me any more," wept Achilles. "Just because I'm hungry and I've got too big. I don't mean to eat up things. They look so delicious, and I'm always starving. Please help me, Sam."

"I don't know how to help you," explained Sam.

"But you're clever," said Achilles. "You can read and add up."

"We'd better go home," said Sam, "and see if Blackbeard Smith's back from holiday. Maybe he can suggest something."

But Blackbeard Smith was still away.

"You'll have to go in the tool shed," said Sam. "I'm really sorry, Achilles. Wait here and I'll get the key. I daren't risk taking you inside."

For Achilles was now taller than Sam.

"I'm scared of the dark," muttered Achilles.

"I'll bring you my torch," promised Sam, "and tomorrow I'll try to think of something to do."

By the time Sam got back with the key and the torch, Achilles had eaten the incinerator that was kept beside the shed, and was another fifteen centimetres taller.

"Kiss me goodnight," begged the parrot.

"I can't reach your beak," said Sam sadly.

With a lot of creaks and clangs, Achilles

bent down. Sam kissed his beak and went inside to bed.

He tossed and turned all night long and slept very badly.

Next day he decided not to go to school.

"I've got a very sore throat," he told his aunt.

"Measles, I expect," she said grimly. "Well, I'm going out this morning. You'll have to stay here by yourself."

Sam was overjoyed. It would make getting the parrot out of the garden much simpler.

But where could he put Achilles? He went out to the tool shed as soon as his aunt had left.

Achilles was delighted to see him and stroked Sam's head with his metal wing.

"You've thought of something?" he creaked hopefully.

"Well, not exactly. I'm just sorting something out," said Sam untruthfully. "First, we have to get you out of the garden."

He draped the coat round Achilles and pulled the cap low down over his beak, then together they set off down the street. Sam had no idea where he was going, but headed vaguely in the direction of the park. Suddenly, ahead of them, Sam saw a policeman. Quick as a flash, he pulled Achilles down on to a low brick wall and sat beside him.

"Keep your head down," he hissed.

The policeman stopped and looked at them with mild interest.

"Good morning," he said.

"Good morning," creaked Achilles.

"It's my grandpa," said Sam desperately. "He's got a bad chest."

"What a shame," said the sympathetic policeman, and walked on.

Then, as Sam sat racking his brains, he had a sudden wonderful idea!

"Get up quickly, Achilles, we're going to the park."

They got to the park and Sam looked cautiously round for a suitable spot.

"Over there," he decided.

He took Achilles to an empty space amongst the trees, pulled off the coat and told the parrot to take off the cap.

"Now just stand there," ordered Sam.

"But everyone will see me," objected Achilles.

"*Exactly!*" cried Sam. "They'll think you're a piece of park sculpture. You're quite safe here and I can go away and try to sort out something. Now, you must promise to stay right here."

"Yes."

"And you won't move away?"

"I promise."

"Good," said Sam. "I'll be back in about an hour."

And he set off to find a solution.

He wandered round the streets for a long time trying to think of something, but by the time he returned to the park he still had no idea what to do about Achilles.

As he got nearer the open space where he had left the parrot, he noticed a crowd of people gathering. Feeling rather uneasy, he pushed his way through.

Achilles was still standing where Sam had left him, but he had clearly been away. Out of his head gushed a bright jet of water. While Sam had been gone, he had eaten the park fountain!

"But that sculpture wasn't there yester-day," insisted a woman at the front of the crowd.

"Keep still," hissed Sam to Achilles. "Stand still."

"I *am* standing still," said the man next door to Sam.

The crowd continued to argue about the new statue. Things were becoming rather heated when there was a sudden shout from behind them.

"Look out! Look out! Danger!"

Sam couldn't see what was going on, but the voice continued.

"Run, run, the new electronic mechanical digger's gone out of control and it's heading this way!"

The crowd of people scattered in all directions.

Sam looked at Achilles.

"Put me on your shoulder," he ordered. "Hurry!"

Achilles lifted Sam in his beak and set him on his shoulder.

The digger was quite far off but advancing quickly. You could see where it had been by the trail it was cutting through the park. As Sam watched, it veered to the left, tore down the park gates, and set off along the street, ripping up large chunks of the road as it went. People ran screaming away from it.

"What is it?" asked Achilles.

"It's a digger," explained Sam, "and its electronic brain has gone wrong."

"It looks *delicious*," said Achilles. "And I'm starving again."

And with Sam clinging to his neck feathers, he lumbered off after the digger.

As they went along, Sam realized in horror that the digger was heading out of the park and towards his own street.

Achilles, who was getting hungrier and hungrier, ran faster and faster.

"I wish that pirate had made me with longer wings, and I could fly," he panted.

As they drew closer, Sam saw that the digger had begun to swerve and that it was tearing up the fence round his aunt and uncle's garden.

Aunt Hilda leant out of the top-floor window, shouting and screaming.

"Help, help! I'll be killed! It's coming straight for me. Oh help, someone!"

The digger dug up the rose garden. It was coming towards the house.

"Hurry, hurry, Achilles!" cried Sam.

Achilles leapt forward on his enormous feet. He opened his great beak.

CRUNCH!

He bit off the digger's metal jaws.

CRUNCH! CRUNCH!

He bit off the digger's mechanical arm.

CRUNCH! CRUNCH! CRUNCH!

He gobbled up the digger's caterpillar tracks and half of the empty cab.

And while Aunt Hilda watched in astonishment, he chewed up all the rest of it.

The mechanical digger was completely eaten up.

"Sam," said Achilles, "that was the best meal I've eaten yet. I have to sit down to digest it."

Aunt Hilda threw open the window.

"Is that you, Sam?" she called.

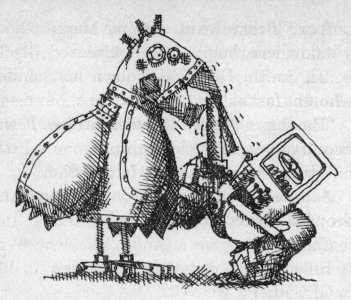

Sam's heart sank.

"Yes," he answered nervously.

"You wonderful, clever, amazing boy," cried Aunt Hilda. "You've saved my life!"

She rushed out of the door and ran across the garden.

"Oh, Sam, how can I ever thank you enough?" she cried gratefully. "You're to choose anything you want, anything at all."

Just at that moment, there came the sound of a familiar voice.

"Is anybody at home to greet the Terror of the Tearing Tea-clippers?" it shouted. "Come out, or I'll carve ye up with me hook."

And there, behind Sam, appeared Black-beard Smith. He looked down at Achilles who was fast asleep after his enormous meal.

"Having a little trouble, are we?" he enquired genially. "Something gone a little bit wrong somewhere, has it, then?"

And taking an oil can in his hook he dropped three drops on to Achilles' tail feathers, adjusted a knob somewhere in Achilles' chest and turned a screw in his head feathers.

There was a clanging and grinding and a sudden rushing clunk! And Achilles shrank back to his old size.

"Oh, Blackbeard!" cried Sam. "He's normal again. He's fixed."

"Quite himself, I can tell you," muttered the pirate. "Been eating, has he?"

"Everything, just everything," Sam said. "And there was nothing I could do."

He bent down and picked up Achilles in his arms.

"He's cured now," said Blackbeard Smith. "It won't happen again, ye may be sure."

At that moment Aunt Hilda, who had been inspecting the damaged fence, noticed the pirate.

"Mr Smith," she said, with a warm smile. "How was your holiday? I'm delighted to see you back. We do miss your services in the garden, you know."

Blackbeard Smith looked hard at Sam.

"This brave boy," continued Aunt Hilda, "has just saved me from a frightful death. I was lying down with a headache when I heard a terrible noise and saw that dreadful machine coming straight at the house."

"Cured your headache, ma'am, without doubt," murmured Blackbeard Smith.

"I shall never have a headache again," said Aunt Hilda decidedly. "And Sam is to choose anything he wants as a reward."

"Anything?" asked Sam.

"Anything at all," answered his aunt.

"Choose carefully now, boy," said the pirate.

"Well," said Sam, thinking hard, "first, I'd like to be allowed friends to tea, and friends *I* choose."

"Of course," said Aunt Hilda.

"Then," Sam went on, "I want to be allowed to go into Blackbeard Smith's shed any time he says I can."

"Certainly," replied Aunt Hilda.

"And, last of all, I want to be allowed as many pets as I want."

Aunt Hilda swallowed hard.

"Well . . ." she said.

"You promised," Sam reminded her.

"Yes," said Aunt Hilda, "I did promise. And you can. I shall speak to Uncle George about it tonight."

"Very lucky that. Nice piece of timing there," said Blackbeard Smith. "Because it just so happens I brought the young hero a little present from Jamaica."

And he pulled a box out of his coat pocket.

Sam opened the box. Inside was a tortoise.

"Oh, Blackbeard!" cried Sam. "I've always wanted a tortoise."

"And one or two other things," said the pirate, "which we'll deal with later. Meanwhile here's a shell which sings if you hold it to your ear."

"It is a rather beautiful tortoise," said Aunt Hilda. "I feel I could probably get to like it in time. But I do think we should go inside now and have some tea."

"Aunt Hilda," said Sam, "I've decided to ask someone to tea today."

"Today?" said his aunt.

"Yes, today," repeated Sam. "I want Blackbeard Smith to come to tea."

"Of course, dear," said his aunt. "Mr Smith will be very welcome."

They went into the kitchen and sat down at the table.

"Sam," said Aunt Hilda, "as it's such a special day today and you have a friend to tea, I've decided to go out and buy ice cream and cake."

"Oh, thank you," cried Sam, and he gave Aunt Hilda a kiss.

Aunt Hilda was very pleased. She took her purse and went out.

Blackbeard Smith and Sam were left alone together. Achilles was still asleep on Sam's shoulder. Sam's tortoise was sitting on his knee.

"It's been a busy time, I see," remarked the retired pirate.

"I've been waiting every day for you to come back," said Sam.

"Sorry ye've had so much trouble with him, boy," said the pirate. "But he's all right now."

"Blackbeard," said Sam, "have you ever owned a dog?"

"Dog?" The pirate looked interested. "Of course I've had a dog. A sea-faring dog that was tied to the mast in the storms of the Indian Ocean. There's nothing about dogs Blackbeard Smith don't know. Remarkable dog I had, and many's the time Cocky Smart rode on his back."

"Do you think I could train Achilles to ride on a dog's back if I had one?"

"Undeniably, boy. That bird can be trained to do anything."

"When I get my dog, Blackbeard," asked Sam, "will you show me how to train him?"

Blackbeard rested his hook on Sam's shoulder. "Without doubt, boy. Without doubt. We'll begin discussing it right away."

And they were still discussing it when Aunt Hilda came back with the ice cream and cake, a bottle of rum for Blackbeard Smith, and a packet of birdseed for Achilles.

"A kind thought, ma'am," said the pirate, "but that bird don't touch birdseed. A few drops of 3-in-1 oil will do him fine."

Achilles opened his eyes and looked around hungrily.

Aunt Hilda went to the cupboard under the sink, took out the bicycle oil, put a little in her saucer and gave it to him.

Achilles looked at Sam.

"Can I?"

"Can he?" Sam asked Blackbeard.

"Of course he can," said the pirate. "Cocky Smart's favourite tipple is marshmallow-flavoured coconut oil."

Achilles dipped his beak into the saucer and gave a deep sigh of contentment.

"You know something?" Sam said to Blackbeard and Aunt Hilda. "However many pets I get, my favourite will always be Achilles."

And Achilles snuggled comfortably into Sam's neck and lovingly pecked his ear.

An Overcrowded House

Adèle Geras

In the entrance hall of my grandmother's flat, there was a cupboard set so high up in the wall that only a tall person standing on a chair could open it. Luckily, my grandmother needed what was kept up there once a year only, so it had to be reached on two occasions: once to bring out the Passover dishes ready for the Festival, every spring, and the second time to put them all away for another twelve months. My tallest cousin, Arieh, was always the person who had to stand on the chair and pass down dishes and cups and plates, knives and forks and pots and pans and glasses to my grandmother and me, waiting to carry them to the kitchen.

At Passover time, all the ordinary dishes were put away and the whole flat was cleaned from top to bottom. Not a single crumb was allowed to lurk forgotten in the corner. Holes in the wall had to be plastered over. Sometimes, my grandmother decided that this or that room needed whitewashing, and she would pile all the furniture into the middle of the room for a day, and cover it with sheets, and then slap a thick, white sloppy brush up and down the walls.

"Why do you have the best things hidden away in the cupboard all the time?" I asked my grandmother. "Why are they only allowed down into the house for a week?"

"Because it's a special celebration," said my grandmother. "It's to celebrate the escape of the Jews from their captivity in Egypt. We will read the whole story again, on the night of the First Seder."

For the Seder the door between the dining room and the room where the long, blue sofa was, was folded back, and the table was pulled out to its full length. More than twenty people would sit around it for the Passover meal, eating matzos and bitter herbs and drinking sweet wine, and telling the story of the Plagues that God sent down to the land of Egypt. In the Hagadah, the book we looked at as the meal continued, there were coloured drawings of the Plagues: frogs, locusts, boils, and a very frightening picture showing a dead child covered in blood, and representing the Death of the First Born. There was also a picture of Moses parting the Red Sea, with high, blue waves towering about the heads of the Israelites like walls of sapphire. We sang songs, and waited up till late at night to see whether this year, the prophet Elijah would come and drink the glass of wine my grandmother always put out for him. At the end of the meal, my cousins and I would run all over the flat searching for the Afikoman. This was half a matzo, wrapped in a napkin, which my grandmother hid like a treasure. Whoever found it won a small prize: an apple or a square of chocolate. There were so many cousins rushing about that I never managed to find the Afikoman, but my grandmother gave us all apples and chocolate too, so I didn't mind.

"It's not very fair for the winner, though," I said to my grandmother. "It makes winning less special."

"Nonsense," said my grandmother. "Finding the Afikoman is an honour and it brings good luck. And looking all over the place is fun, too."

In spite of the special dishes, and the book with pictures of the Plagues, in spite of the sips of sweet wine and the brown-freckled matzos which tasted so delicious with strawberry jam on them, I was always quite glad when the festival was over and the visitors went home. Then I could have my grandmother to myself again and she could tell me stories.

"You don't know," she said, "how well off you are. I should tell you the story of Mordechai and Chaya. Once upon a time, there was a farmer called Mordechai, who lived in a miserable little farmhouse right on the edge of the village. He had two muddy fields next to the house, where he tried to grow this and that and the other. I have to tell you that most of the time he failed miserably, and when Chaya took the farm produce to the market and set it out on a stall, people walked by with their noses in the air saying: 'Pshaw! Such cabbages I wouldn't feed to my chickens! Do you call this a turnip? This is a turnip's wizened grandfather! And this is not a potato, this is a joke . . .' and so forth. But Chaya didn't laugh. The money grew scarcer and scarcer, and the couple grew more and more miserable. Then, one terrible day, Mordechai's father died, leaving Mordechai's mother penniless. She had to sell her house to pay her late husband's debts, and so there she was, homeless at her age. Well, there was no alternative: the poor old lady had to move in at once with Mordechai and Chaya. It was difficult to know quite where to put her. The farmhouse was really two rooms: one large room, with a corner curtained off to hide the bed where Mordechai and Chaya slept, and one tiny room which the couple called the kitchen, but which could more accurately have been called a cupboard with a window. When Mordechai's mother moved in, he hung a curtain across another corner of the large room, to hide the bed she had brought with her, and tried to make the best of it. But it was difficult.

'What shall we do?' he asked Chaya. 'She snores at night and keeps me awake.'

'She squeezes into the kitchen to help me cook,' said Chaya, 'so that I can hardly move. I think you should go and see the Rabbi. Ask his advice.'

'What good will that do?' asked Mordechai.

'What harm will it do?' his wife replied.

So in the end, Mordechai went to the Rabbi and told him all his troubles. This Rabbi was not as clever as Rabbi Samuels, but he wasn't a fool. He listened to Mordechai, and muttered and mumbled into his beard, and fixed his eyes on an interesting spot on the ceiling, and finally he turned to Mordechai.

'Have you any livestock?' he asked.

'A few chickens . . . a goat . . . a cow to give milk . . . nothing much, I assure you.'

'Take the chickens,' said the Rabbi, 'and move them into the house with you.'

'Into the house?' Mordechai thought the Rabbi had gone mad.

'Exactly,' said the Rabbi. 'Do as I say and your troubles will soon be over.'

Mordechai did as the Rabbi said. Never had he and Chaya been so miserable. The chickens squawked all day and got under everyone's feet. They laid eggs in unexpected places and flew on to the table at mealtimes to share what little food there was. The rooster had decided that Mordechai and Chaya's brass bedstead was his perch, and there, every morning, he would split the dawn in half with his crowing. Mordechai and Chaya used to leap out of their skins in fright.

'Go back to the Rabbi,' said Chaya. 'Tell him everything is ten times worse than before.'

So Mordechai went and poured out all his woes to the Rabbi. The Rabbi muttered and mumbled into his beard and fixed his eyes on an interesting spot on the back of the door, and then finally he turned to Mordechai.

'You said you had a cow?' he asked.

'Yes . . . one cow.'

'Bring the cow into the house,' said the Rabbi.

'Where will I put her?'

'Tie her up to the handle of the door,' said the Rabbi. 'All your troubles will soon be over.'

Mordechai returned to the farmhouse and told his wife what the Rabbi had said.

'He has taken leave of his senses,' said Chaya. 'But he is an educated man, so we should at least try it.'

Life immediately went from bad to worse. No one could move in or out of the door without bumping into the cow. Twice, she pulled the rickety door off its hinges, and once chewed up both the curtain hiding Mordechai's mother's bed and some of her blankets as well.

'Go back to the Rabbi,' said Chaya after a week had passed. 'Tell him everything is a hundred times worse than before.'

So Mordechai went and cried out his anguish to the Rabbi. The Rabbi muttered and mumbled into his beard and fixed his eyes on an interesting spot on the floor, and then finally he turned to Mordechai.

'Do you still have a goat?'

'Yes . . . one goat.'

'Bring the goat into the house.'

'Where will I put him?'

'Tie him up to the end of your bed,' said the Rabbi, 'and your troubles will soon be over.'

Mordechai returned to the farmhouse. When he told Chaya what the Rabbi had said, she couldn't believe her ears.

'The Rabbi is bewitched,' she cried. 'What is he telling us to do? Look at my house. Look what he has made us do already . . . there are chickens wherever you look, clucking and squawking and dropping eggs and feathers all over the floor, the cow knocks over all the furniture and pulls the door off its hinges, my linen drawer has become a manger full of straw, and now he wants us to bring in the goat as well . . . and tie him to the end of our bed. It's too much!' She sat down at the table and wept salty tears into the dough she had been kneading.

'But you said yourself,' said Mordechai, 'he is an educated man, and so we should at least try it.' So Chaya wiped her tears away and went to fetch the goat.

The next day, Chaya went with Mordechai to see the Rabbi. They sat at the table and Chaya spoke first.

'My husband has been to you before,' she

said, 'and you have advised him and we have followed your advice. Yesterday you told us to bring in the goat, and we did it, and today we are both three-quarters of the way to our graves. It wasn't the fact that the goat ate every single thing it could reach, including a piece from my husband's nightshirt. After all, what do I own that's too precious for a goat to eat? Nothing, that's what. No, Rabbi, what finally drove us to seek your help is the stench. Have you ever slept within three feet of a goat? I thought my last hour had come. We have not slept a wink all night. Tell us, Rabbi, what do we do now?'

The Rabbi did not mutter, nor did he mumble. He did not fix his eyes on interesting spots anywhere in the room. Instead, he spoke straight to Mordechai and Chaya.

'Take the goat and the cow and the chickens out of your house. Return them to their own quarters. Then clean your house from top to bottom, and come and tell me how you feel.'

Two days later, Mordechai and Chaya

returned to the Rabbi's house.

'Oh, thank you, thank you, Rabbi,' they said. 'Our house is restored to us. It is clean and quiet and it doesn't smell of goat!'

'But what about Mordechai's mother? Do you not find it crowded?' said the Rabbi.

'Crowded?' said Mordechai. 'It's like a palace.'

'Paradise!' agreed Chaya. 'I shall never complain about it ever again.'

And she never did."

Pappy Mashy

Kathy Henderson

Pappy Mashy always sat in the armchair.
It was the only comfortable chair. It
was the only chair he could fit into. And he
always read the newspaper.

The Mashy children – Josie, Rosie,
Gemma, Lisa, Tracy, Lacey, Wayne, Elaine
and little Arbuthnot Mashy – played mostly.

And Mammy Mashy did everything else.

She fed the cats,
shook the mats,
cooked the meals,
hushed the squeals,
kept bees,
pruned trees,
taught the children their *abc*s,
fixed the roof,

unblocked the drains,

nursed the children's aches and pains,

ironed,

washed,

knitted,

sewed,

sang songs,

wrote letters,

changed nappies,

paid bills,

went to the supermarket,

mended punctures,

and read the bedtime story.

And when the older children were all safe in the classrooms of Sloth Road School, the baby was with Lilly-next-door and Pappy Mashy had stumbled off to his office to turn over more papers at his desk all day, then she'd go out to her part-time job as a bus driver.

But she always made sure she was home in time to collect the children and say hello to Pappy as he sank into his armchair to read the evening papers.

Of course.

"Leave him be," she'd say to the little ones as she cooked the supper with one hand and did the big ones' homework with the other. "Your father's had a hard day."

That was just the way things were.

Now, though he was fat, it wasn't that Pappy Mashy was a lazy man. It was just that he liked to read the newspaper. And over the years, as his family had grown larger and larger, so he had come to like reading the newspapers more and more.

By the time little Arbuthnot was born, Pappy Mashy didn't just read one newspaper like most people. He didn't just read two newspapers like some people. He read lots of newspapers. In fact he read every newspaper he could lay his hands on. There was:

The Smellygraph
The Chimes
The Despondent
The Daily Excess

There was:

The Flash
The Stars
The Morning Shout
The Evening Screech

And that was just to start with. You name it, he read it, from the first page to the last, every single word.

Pappy Mashy read so many newspapers that the paper-boy from the shop down the road had got a bad case of soggy legs from carrying them all and refused to deliver to number 23 any more.

So now, very early every morning, the Mashys' front door would open and out would come Josie, Rosie, Gemma, Lisa, Tracy, Lacey, Wayne, Elaine and little Arbuthnot, and they'd trot down the road to the newspaper shop and stagger back with a newspaper under each and every arm.

And though Pappy Mashy was too busy reading to play with them, too busy reading to talk to them, too busy reading even to notice them, it wasn't that he didn't love his children. It was only that he couldn't resist the comfortable chair and the pile of newspapers.

The Mashy children were a clever lot and as busy as bees. They helped their mum. They helped their dad, and they certainly stood out at school.

Wayne and Elaine had nursery class helper badges for looking after the gerbils.

Tracy and Lacey loved dressing up.

Gemma specialized in weather forecasting.

Josie could do the crossword faster than her teacher, and knew more long words.

Lisa was into art and craft; and Arbuthnot showed every sign of taking after his father.

And Rosie? Rosie with the red hair and the bright blue eyes was the cleverest of them all. She noticed things.

Now as the winter wore away and spring drew near, Rosie did a lot of noticing.

She noticed that Mammy was getting thinner and thinner, while Pappy was getting fatter and fatter (so fat indeed that he could scarcely fit into the comfortable chair any

more). And she noticed that Mammy was getting snappier and snappier, while Pappy was getting snoozier and snoozier.

So Rosie at least was not surprised when one morning Mammy Mashy just couldn't get up.

"I'm sorry," she said, lying there in her bed, and her face was pale pale pale, "I'b got a code id by dose ad an ache id by head ad I feel terrible."

Pappy Mashy was very worried. "I'm going to call the doctor," he said and thumped downstairs.

"Don't worry," said Josie. "We'll manage between us, won't we?"

"Yes," said Rosie, Gemma, Lisa, Tracy, Lacey, Wayne and Elaine in a chorus. Arbuthnot chuckled. "So stay in bed and have a good rest," said Rosie, leading them out.

A little while later Dr Porridge came to see Mammy Mashy. She spent a long time with her. On her way out she gave Pappy and the children their instructions: "She's to spend a week in bed," said Dr Porridge firmly. "A *whole* week. She's not to work, not to be worried, she's not even to come downstairs. What she needs is lots of warm drinks and peace and quiet and sleep. Is that clear?"

Josie, Rosie, Gemma, Lisa, Tracy, Lacey, Wayne, Elaine and little Arbuthnot all nodded solemnly. Even Pappy Mashy nodded, but his eyes were sliding towards the pages of the *Isfahan Gazette*.

It was a desperate week.

Josie, Rosie, Gemma, Lisa, Tracy, Lacey, Wayne and Elaine worked like slaves, but no matter how hard they worked, still the dirty dishes piled up and the food supplies ran down and the drains got blocked and little Arbuthnot did unspeakable things when they weren't looking. And the tide of old newspapers rose and rose and swilled around the house threatening to engulf them all.

Pappy Mashy did try. He got up in the morning. He went to bed at night. He carried trays of warm drinks up to Mammy. He even fetched his own newspapers. But it took no more than a glimpse of his armchair for him to need a little read. And the little reads grew longer and longer until he was buried there almost as much as he had ever been.

"This will not *do*!" said Rosie to Josie on Thursday night, as they swept a mountain of old paper out into the back yard.

"I'll give you a hand when I've finished this," mumbled Pappy Mashy sheepishly from the depths of the comfortable chair.

Lacey was cross. "Humph!" she snorted. "He's just like the man in the story Mrs

Bugwort told us at school, the man who was turned into stone."

"Except it's not stone he's been turned to," said Rosie, "it's newspaper!"

By Friday they had eaten scrambled eggs six nights in a row, so Josie made pancake batter instead.

There was a gloomy silence in the kitchen, and they could hear the sound of Pappy sinking deeper into his papers next door.

"If only we could get him out of his chair," said Rosie.

"We had Miss Gullet for craft yesterday," piped up Lisa from the doorway.

"Really, Lisa, is that all you can think about!" fretted Josie.

"Look out!" Elaine and Wayne staggered in with a pile of dirty washing. Wayne heaved it into the washing machine. Elaine lifted the box of soap out on to the worktop.

"And we did papiyaay machaay," went on Lisa, unconcerned, "and Miss Gullet says there's going to be a craft competition and that I should make something for it."

Just then, Arbuthnot emptied a bag of flour on to the floor with spectacular results. He chortled. The kitchen filled with a cloud of dust and Josie, Rosie and Elaine all threw themselves on the floor to clear up the mess.

Seeing that they were busy, Arbuthnot decided to improve the batter mix. He leant over to the box of soap powder, picked up a scoopful and emptied it into the mixing bowl.

The batter started to froth.

"Oh no!" raged Josie, straightening up, her hair white with flour. "There goes supper and we haven't got any eggs left!"

It was Rosie to the rescue. "No use crying over spilt milk," she said, removing the revolting Arbuthnot to the living room. Then she came back, picked up the mixing bowl and emptied it into the rubbish bin.

Lisa stared into the bin. Then she did something very odd. Instead of putting the lid back on, she reached her hand into the sticky mess of batter and newspaper and stirred.

"*Yuk!*" shrieked Josie. "That's disgusting! What are you doing?" Elaine made sick noises.

Lisa lifted her hand out and let blobs of batter and paper drip.

"It's a bit like Miss Gullet's papiyaay mashaay," she sang to herself with a little smile.

Rosie was noticing. "Now I come to think of it," she said, "I seem to remember we did papier mâché when we were in Miss Gullet's too . . ."

Josie looked at them both as if they were mad.

". . . and you can make models and things with it, can't you?"

"I'm hungry," wailed Wayne.

"All it is, is newspaper and flour-and-water paste, like batter without the eggs," said Lisa.

"And it goes all hard . . . As hard as stone," said Rosie thoughtfully.

"That's it!" she said, picking up a handful of gloop out of the bin. "Bother housework. I know what we're going to do!"

And Rosie danced a war dance on the sticky kitchen floor.

So it was cold baked beans for supper, and Pappy didn't even notice. He was too busy reading the *Bogota Bulletin*.

"We'll clear up, Pappy," said Josie when they'd finished. "You take this hot drink up to Mum and keep her company for the evening." And Pappy, his nose still in his paper, obeyed like a lamb.

Then the fun began.

Such a ripping and tearing, a giggling and a scrunching you never did hear. Every waste-paper basket was emptied, every paper pile was plundered and soon the whole ground floor of number 23 was filled with shreds and strips of torn newspaper.

Out in the kitchen Josie and Gemma beat buckets full of batter.

Arbuthnot played snowstorms in the hall and Rosie and Lisa were hard at work dismantling the old rabbit run and twisting the chicken wire that covered it into a strangely familiar shape.

All night long they worked, pasting and patting, slopping and sticking, while Arbuthnot slept in a nest of cushions.

And when the first blackbird sang from the next door TV aerial, there was not a single newspaper, not even the tiniest shred of newspaper to be seen anywhere.

Josie, Rosie, Gemma, Lisa, Tracy, Lacey, Wayne and Elaine picked up little Arbuthnot and tiptoed upstairs to bed as the first cars revved in the street outside.

When Pappy Mashy staggered downstairs that morning he thought he'd seen a ghost.

It wasn't just that the house was tidy. Nor even that there wasn't a single heap of newspapers to be seen.

It was *that*!

There in his armchair, the only comfortable armchair, in fact the only chair he could fit into nowadays, there was something . . . someone . . . sitting . . . and reading . . . *his* newspaper!

Little Arbuthnot bumped down the stairs and landed at his feet.

231

"Pappy," said Arbuthnot stretching out his arms, and in his amazement Pappy Mashy actually bent down and picked him up! Arbuthnot gurgled happily and clapped his hands and Pappy became aware of a whole circle of sleepy children standing round him.

For the first time in a long time, Pappy Mashy looked straight at his children. They looked back expectantly.

Then, feeling weak at the knees with so much effort, he turned towards his chair again, and groaned.

"Who *is* that?"

"It's *papier mâché!*" said the children in chorus.

"Pappy Mashy?" whimpered Pappy. "But that's me!"

The children giggled. Pappy Mashy went over to the figure in the chair.

"May I have my newspaper?" he asked.

The figure didn't move. Pappy took hold of the newspaper.

It wouldn't move either. So Pappy pulled. The newspaper ripped.

"Well at least let me have my chair!"

Pappy took the figure firmly by the arms. He tugged, he shook, but all that happened was that the chair lifted off the ground. The figure was stuck fast.

And when he dropped it in despair, the whole lot landed on his foot.

Pappy hopped round the room in agony. The children were amazed. They couldn't ever remember him taking so much exercise in one morning.

But Tracy took no notice. "Hey, Pappy," she said. "Come and look at this thing I've made, it's a superstrawbercoopercopter."

Pappy stopped hopping. "Huh?" he said.

And then he did another very unusual thing. Without a newspaper to read or a chair to sit in, Pappy *did* look.

In fact, he did more than look. He bent down and touched. Before long he was vrooming the superstrawbercoopercopter all over the newspaper-free floor. Wonder of wonders, Pappy was playing!

Pappy Mashy was so busy playing that he didn't hear the doorbell. He scarcely noticed Miss Gullet come in, and when he saw Josie and Rosie and Lisa help her carry *his* chair out to the car for the craft exhibition, he was having such a good time playing, that he just shrugged and waved.

"Phew!" he said as he mopped his face. "I haven't enjoyed myself so much for ages! Why don't you ask me to play with you more often?"

And Josie, Rosie, Gemma, Lisa, Tracy, Lacey, Wayne, Elaine and little Arbuthnot all laughed.

That afternoon Mammy Mashy came downstairs for the first time. She was pale and weak but her face seemed rested. The dark lines under her eyes had gone and she looked somehow rounder than before.

"Well, well," she said as she looked around, "you have done a good job!" Pappy smirked as if he'd done it all himself. Josie kicked him. "But where's the big chair gone?"

"Big chair?" asked Pappy, as if he'd never heard of it (and indeed he had almost forgotten it already). "It's er . . ."

"Being redecorated," said Lisa firmly. And

that was the end of that.

But Rosie was noticing as usual. "Are you sure you're all right, Mum?" she said. "You look a bit shaky."

"I do feel a bit weak," admitted Mammy. "I think, if you don't mind, I'll just have a little sit down."

And she sat down in the second most comfortable armchair and opened a book.

ACKNOWLEDGEMENTS

The publishers wish to thank the following for permission to reproduce copyright material:

Margaret Mahy: "The Downhill Crocodile Whizz" from *The Downhill Crocodile Whizz and Other Stories* by Margaret Mahy; first published by J.M. Dent & Sons 1986 and reproduced by permission of the Orion Publishing Group Ltd.

Stephen Corrin: "Clever Stan and the Stupid Dragon" from *A Time to Laugh* edited by Sara and Stephen Corrin; first published by Faber & Faber and reproduced with their permission.

Margaret Joy: "Cup Final" from *You're in the Juniors Now* by Margaret Joy; first published by Faber & Faber Ltd and reproduced with their permission.

Michael Bond: "Paddington Goes Underground" from *A Bear Goes Underground* by Michael Bond; first published by William Collins Sons & Co Ltd and © Michael Bond 1958; reproduced by permission of Lemon Unna and Durbridge Ltd. All rights reserved and all enquiries concerning performance rights to The Agency (London) Ltd, 24 Pottery Lane, London W11 4LZ, Fax: 0207 727 9037.

Ann Cameron: "Julian, Dream Doctor", an extract from *Julian, Dream Doctor* by Ann Cameron; first published by Victor Gollancz Ltd 1992 and reproduced with their permission.

David Henry Wilson: "The Missing Nose" from *Gander of the Yard* by David Henry Wilson; first published by J.M. Dent & Sons Ltd 1989 and reproduced by permission of the Orion Publishing Group Ltd.

Dick King-Smith: *Emily's Legs* by Dick King-Smith; first published by Wayland Publishers Ltd 1988 and reproduced with their permission.

Roger McGough: "The Stowaways" from *The Stowaways* by Roger McGough; first published by Penguin Books 1986 and reproduced by permission of Peters, Fraser & Dunlop Group Ltd.

Diana Hendry: "The Worm Hunt" from *Kid Kibble* by Diana Hendry; Text © 1992 Diana Hendry and originally illustrated by Adriano Gon; first published by Walker Books Ltd and reproduced with their permission.

Philippa Gregory: "Florizella and the Giant", an extract from *Florizella and the Giant* by Philippa Gregory; Text © 1992 Philippa Gregory and originally

ACKNOWLEDGEMENTS

illustrated by Patrice Aggs; first published by Walker Books Ltd and reproduced with their permission.

Jacqueline Wilson: "The Mum-Minder", an extract from *The Mum-Minder* by Jacqueline Wilson; first published by Yearling Books, a division of Transworld Publishers Ltd and © 1993 Jacqueline Wilson. All rights reserved.

Judy Corbalis: "The Magic Parrot" from *The Wrestling Princess and Other Stories* by Judy Corbalis; first published by Andre Deutsch 1986 and reproduced by permission of Scholastic Ltd.

Adèle Geras: "An Overcrowded House" from *My Grandmother's House* by Adèle Geras; first published by William Heinemann Ltd 1990 and reproduced by permission of Reed Consumer Books Ltd.

Kathy Henderson: *Pappy Mashy* by Kathy Henderson; Text © 1992 Kathy Henderson and originally illustrated by Chris Fisher; first published by Walker Books and reproduced with their permission.

Books in this series available from Macmillan

The prices shown below are correct at the time of going to press. However, Macmillan Publishers reserve the right to show new retail prices on covers which may differ from those previously advertised.

Funny Stories for Five Year Olds	0 330 39124 0	£3.99
Magical Stories for Five Year Olds	0 330 39122 4	£3.99
Animal Stories for Five Year Olds	0 330 39125 9	£3.99
Adventure Stories for Five Year Olds	0 330 39137 2	£3.99
Bedtime Stories for Five Year Olds	0 330 48366 8	£3.99
Funny Stories for Six Year Olds	0 330 36857 5	£3.99
Magical Stories for Six Year Olds	0 330 36858 3	£3.99
Animal Stories for Six Year Olds	0 330 36859 1	£3.99
Adventure Stories for Six Year Olds	0 330 39138 0	£3.99
Bedtime Stories for Six Year Olds	0 330 48368 4	£3.99
Funny Stories for Seven Year Olds	0 330 34945 7	£3.99
Magical Stories for Seven Year Olds	0 330 34943 0	£3.99
Animal Stories for Seven Year Olds	0 330 35494 9	£3.99
Adventure Stories for Seven Year Olds	0 330 39139 9	£3.99
Funny Stories for Eight Year Olds	0 330 34946 5	£3.99
Magical Stories for Eight Year Olds	0 330 34944 9	£3.99
Animal Stories for Eight Year Olds	0 330 35495 7	£3.99
Adventure Stories for Eight Year Olds	0 330 39140 2	£3.99
Funny Stories for Nine Year Olds	0 330 37491 5	£3.99
Magical Stories for Nine Year Olds	0 330 37492 3	£3.99
Animal Stories for Nine Year Olds	0 330 37493 1	£3.99
Adventure Stories for Nine Year Olds	0 330 39141 0	£3.99
Funny Stories for Ten Year Olds	0 330 39127 5	£3.99
Magical Stories for Ten Year Olds	0 330 39126 7	£3.99
Animal Stories for Ten Year Olds	0 330 39128 3	£3.99
Adventure Stories for Ten Year Olds	0 330 39142 9	£3.99

All Macmillan titles can be ordered at your local bookshop or are available by post from:
Book Service by Post
PO Box 29, Douglas, Isle of Man IM99 1BQ

Credit cards accepted. For details:
Telephone: 01624 675137
Fax: 01624 670923
E-mail: bookshop@enterprise.net

Free postage and packing in the UK.
Overseas customers: add £1 per book (paperback) and £3 per book (hardback)